OPERATION
TROJAN WAR

INDIGORIVER
PUBLISHING

OPERATION TROJAN WAR

JUSTIN I. PAQUETTE

Operation Trojan War

Editors: Abigail Dengler, Shelby Poulin
Cover and Interior Design: Emma Elzinga

Indigo River Publishing
3 West Garden Street, Ste. 718
Pensacola, FL 32502

www.indigoriverpublishing.com

Ordering Information:

Quantity Sales: Special discounts are available on quantity purchases by corporations, associations, and others. For details, contact the publisher at the address above.

Orders by US trade bookstores and wholesalers: Please contact the publisher at the address above.

Printed in the United States of America

Library of Congress Control Number: 2025920810
ISBN: 978-1-964686-86-8 (paperback)   978-1-964686-87-5 (ebook)

First Edition

With Indigo River Publishing, you can always expect great books, strong voices, and meaningful messages. Most importantly, you'll always find . . . *words worth reading.*

This book is dedicated to my wife and daughter, my family and friends. I love you.

TOP SECRET // SCI

CONTAINS SENSITIVE COMPARTMENTED INFORMATION

THIS IS A COVER SHEET FOR CLASSIFIED INFORMATION.

ALL INDIVIDUALS ARE REQUIRED TO PROTECT THIS INFORMATION FROM UNAUTHORIZED DISCLOSURE IN THE INTEREST OF NATIONAL SECURITY.

HANDLING, STORAGE, REPRODUCTION, AND DISPOSITION OF THE ATTACHED DOCUMENT MUST BE IN ACCORDANCE WITH APPLICABLE EXECUTIVE ORDERS, STATUTES, AND AGENCY IMPLEMENTING REGULATIONS.

TOP SECRET
RESTRICTED DATA

UNAUTHORIZED DISCLOSURE SUBJECT TO ADMINISTRATIVE AND CRIMINAL SANCTIONS

(This cover sheet is unclassified.)

TOP SECRET // SCI

To: **<Redacted Information>**
From: **<Redacted Information>**
Subject: Operation Trojan War

Date: **<Redacted Information>**
Notice: The enclosed document package is classified:
TOP SECRET/SECURE

COMPARTMENTED INFORMATION

To Whom It May Concern

On behalf of **<Redacted Information>**, please accept the following classified document package.

The enclosed classified document package pertains to Operation Trojan War.

Operation Trojan War is approximated to have occurred over the following dates and times: **<Redacted Information>** to **<Redacted Information>**.

Operation Trojan War is believed to have occurred in the following known and/or suspected locations and possibly involved the following known and/or suspected persons: **<Redacted Information>**.

For ease of reading, this classified document package is formatted as a "clean copy" audio transcript of the debriefing interrogation. This classified debriefing transcript is divided into thirty (30) separate sections and twelve (12) attachments for current and future investigative and legal purposes.

Unauthorized disclosure and/or dissemination of this classified document package is a felony and is prohibited under law. Violation is punishable by imprisonment, fines, or both.

Respectfully submitted,

<Redacted Information>

START TRANSCRIPT

SECTION 1

INTERVIEWER / INTERROGATOR

You are being debriefed as part of a classified follow-up investigation regarding your involvement in a restricted access program and operation designated as Operation Trojan War. Do you understand?

SUBJECT

Yes.

INTERVIEWER / INTERROGATOR

All specific dates and times have been sealed, redacted, or otherwise purged from any databases or open sources of information. All locations in which these events are believed to have occurred have also been sealed, redacted, or otherwise purged. All the names of people alive, dead, or missing who were or are believed to be involved in Operation Trojan War have also been sealed, redacted, or otherwise purged from any databases or other open sources of information. Your name has also been redacted. Do you understand?

SUBJECT

Yes.

INTERVIEWER / INTERROGATOR

No publicly available record exists in any way, shape, or form. Nothing discussed, discovered, or disclosed here is subject to any freedom of information request or right-to-know laws in any of the assumed locations of these events. This protected information includes, but is not limited to, any tactics, techniques, or procedures believed to have been used at any time during Operation Trojan War. Do you understand?

SUBJECT

I do.

INTERVIEWER / INTERROGATOR

This matter is classified at the highest possible level and considered a national security matter. Any dissemination of these events, or discovery by our enemies or citizens, has been determined to be a clear and present danger to our nation. Do you understand?

SUBJECT

I understand.

INTERVIEWER / INTERROGATOR

You have agreed to be interviewed and debriefed as an involved participant and a cooperating witness in exchange for complete immunity against any criminal charges and civil lawsuits, provided that the presented information is nothing but the whole truth, containing no willful acts of omission or misrepresentations. Is this true?

SUBJECT

Yes.

INTERVIEWER / INTERROGATOR

You have also been provided these terms in writing and have had ample opportunity to review these documents with competent legal counsel, provided to you at no cost. I am also looking at a signed affidavit acknowledging your receipt, understanding, and agreement to the terms and conditions in these documents. Is this still true, as well?

SUBJECT

It is.

INTERVIEWER / INTERROGATOR

From this point forward in our debriefing, I will address you by your operational call sign, Muse. You will use my operational call sign, Homer. Are you ready to begin?

MUSE

I guess I don't have much of a choice, do I?

HOMER

You always have a choice. You can always refuse to cooperate. But if you refuse to participate, you'll go to prison. It's not a great choice, but it is a choice.

MUSE

I guess so.

HOMER

I also want to be clear on certain points: your involvement in the following events was not the result of threats or coercion. Instead, you acted in these events of your own free will. Do you agree or disagree with these points?

MUSE

I agree.

HOMER

Now, you are being presented with an option, a way out. All that is being asked of you is that you fully and truthfully cooperate so we can figure out what happened and why it happened. So, I'll ask you one last time. Yes or no, are you ready to begin?

MUSE

Yeah, let's begin. What do you want to know?

HOMER

I want you to tell me about Achilles. I want to know what went down and why it went down. I want to understand what led Achilles to leave a trail of bodies and destruction in his wake. I want to know why Zeus allowed that destruction.

SECTION 2

MUSE

You're fixating on the wrong thing. I'll get to Achilles, but he's not as big a player in this shitshow as you think he is. First, we have to start at the beginning.

HOMER

Okay. Let's start at the beginning. What can you tell me?

MUSE

This whole situation spiraled out of control because of a personal beef between Agamemnon and Priam Their hatred for one another was well-known and never-ending within the private contracting community. But even that conflict was only a small part of the overall situation.

HOMER

Then tell me about the bigger parts.

MUSE

This mess, that we now know as Operation Trojan War, all began when a freelance private intelligence operative obtained extremely embarrassing and compromising information on Zeus.

HOMER

Who was the operative? And what was his name?

MUSE

The operative wasn't a him. The operative was a her. And she went by the name Helen Argos.

HOMER

Go on.

MUSE

The short version is that Helen acquired dirt on Zeus and then used that information in an attempt to blackmail him, to ensure his silence.

HOMER

What's the long version?

MUSE

Helen shopped this compromising information around to the highest bidder. Zeus knew that his political career, his power, and his influence would be over if his main political rival, Hera, discovered or acquired it.

HOMER

Sounds like Zeus was forced to make a decision.

MUSE

He was, and he decided to take matters into his own hands by orchestrating an off-the-books capture-or-kill operation. But here's the rub: he couldn't use conventional sources, means, or methods . . . white side or black side. He had to go outside, so he contracted the job to the two largest private contracting entities, Hoplite and Trojan..

HOMER

And you were part of this off-the-books operation, right?

MUSE

No. Not me. Not directly.

HOMER

How do you figure? The way I see the situation, you played both ends against the middle.

MUSE

No. I didn't. Believe it or not, I've actually worked for both Hoplite and Trojan, and both companies were aware that I've worked for the other.

HOMER

How did you manage to pull that off?

MUSE

Simple. I'm honest and upfront about who I am and what I do.

HOMER

And for the record, what do you do?

MUSE

I run a private intelligence company.

HOMER

And what does that job entail?

MUSE

I observe, gather, analyze, and report my findings. Nothing more. My work isn't directly kinetic. So, what I find out for one client only gets reported to that client, and what I gather for another client only gets reported to that client. I won't act as a double or triple agent.

HOMER

Why not?

MUSE

Double-crossing is bad for business—and even worse for your life expectancy.

HOMER

Companies like Trojan and Hoplite don't have their own intel shops or intelligence-gathering capabilities?

MUSE

They do, but their in-house options provide different services than what I provide—and what Helen provided.

HOMER

I don't completely understand. Can you explain further?

MUSE

Look, what I do and what I'm talking about is private sector stuff. This isn't big government bullshit with a bottomless bucket of cash where you just constantly throw good money after bad until the problem goes away. What I do is more cost-effective and efficient. My services aren't cheap, and Helen charges even more than I do. But in the long run, companies like Hoplite and Trojan spend less if they subcontract out certain aspects rather than trying to do the job themselves. The same holds for governments. Could they do the job themselves? Sure, but their involvement always runs the risk of being leaked and becoming public knowledge. If Hoplite or Trojan fucked up, they couldn't come back from that fuck up easily.

HOMER

But that rule doesn't apply to you?

MUSE

Let's look at this situation another way. I'm a specialist. Helen even more so. I provide a full-service suite of intelligence: human, signal, electronic, and rumor. I will use human case officers, agents, and analysts, but my trademark, my specialty, is my use of remotely operated platforms.

HOMER

Such as?

MUSE

Air, land, and sea-capable, unmanned vehicles. Drones. I offer one-stop shopping with confidentiality and exclusivity guaranteed. And my only rule, as I've said before, is that I do not do anything kinetic. I don't do wet work of any kind.

HOMER

So, you find and fix, but the client finishes? Is that how this works? None of the consequences fall on you?

MUSE

What a client does with the intelligence I provide is one hundred percent on them.

HOMER

What about Helen?

MUSE

What about her?

HOMER

How did she operate?

MUSE

She is on a completely different level.

HOMER

How so?

MUSE

She isn't just a person. Helen is an idea, Helen is a concept, and Helen is more than just a singleton operative. What she runs is a network—a conglomerate of like-minded individuals operating in a very similar fashion to how Agamemnon set up Hoplite.

HOMER

Explain.

MUSE

Take my company, Fate, for example. I deal with raw data and information, right? As I've said before, I obtain raw data and information through observation, collection, analysis, and interpretation. I then report what I have to my client, and my client uses those findings as they see fit. What I do is pretty straightforward.

HOMER

But Helen's style isn't this simple?

MUSE

No. Her operation is almost exclusively based on information collected by human sources from human sources, whereas I'll run the spectrum on intelligence-gathering methods. Helen might pull some stuff from computers, phones, emails, text messages, or other shit like that; but she relies on old-school tradecraft like person-to-person interactions. These kinds of methods rank low in sophistication but high in efficiency.

HOMER

I'm still not completely following you.

MUSE

Let me guess. You're struggling to understand how someone—without relying heavily on technology—could gather enough intel to take down the most powerful person on the planet. Is that right?

HOMER

Yeah, that's exactly it.

MUSE

Helen used a method known as MISE.

HOMER

Mice? Like rodents?

MUSE

No, man. It's an acronym.

HOMER

Can you explain what the acronym means, for the record?

MUSE

Sure, but there are two variations.

HOMER

What are they?

MUSE

The first and most common variation is MICE with a C, which stands for money, ideology, compromise, and ego.

HOMER

The second?

MUSE

Helen excels at the second variation. This version is MISE with an S, which stands for money, ideology, sex, and ego. The two acronyms are basically the same, but these are the weaknesses and proclivities that Helen looks for. When she finds them, she uses them to leverage, exploit, and even blackmail her target. What she does is risky and dangerous.

HOMER

How?

MUSE

Remember what I said earlier, about me being upfront and honest if I'm employed by two competing clients? And about how double-crossing is bad for business and worse for life expectancy?

HOMER

Yes, but what does that have to do with Helen?

MUSE

Helen doesn't give a shit about that stuff. She doesn't give a fuck about who she screws over, as long as she gets paid. But this time, she fucked someone who could fuck her back. Zeus was the biggest target she'd ever gone after. In comparison, all her other targets were small potatoes. She mostly targeted celebrities, business executives, athletes, and state-level politicians. Maybe she'd go for low-level house representatives and senators, but nobody as big as Zeus.

HOMER

Then why go after him?

MUSE

Why not? What's that old adage? If you want to be the best, you should go after the best?

HOMER

I think it's "beat" the best, but what you're saying is true. But there's another adage. If you take a shot at the king, you better not miss. Helen missed.

MUSE

She didn't completely miss. She winged him. She definitely over-extended herself on this one, but she largely accomplished what she set out to do.

HOMER

Which was?

MUSE

Hers was every grifter's dream—hitting that one big score and then walking away. She could cement her legend and ride off into the proverbial sunset. If she pulled this off, her organization could go on, but she'd no longer have to operate.

HOMER

Speaking of operating, what are her procedures? Do you know her means, methods, tactics, techniques?

MUSE

She uses a pairing as old as time itself: sex and ego. Use and control those two things, and you can manipulate your mark's ideology and get them to do whatever you want.

HOMER

But Helen couldn't have possibly been sexually involved with every single mark?

MUSE

She wasn't. Remember, Helen was a network, a concept, and an idea. She was personally involved with some of them, like with Zeus. But for other marks, she utilized other operatives. Men, women, transexuals—whatever people are into. Whatever blows their hair back. Rest assured, Helen had what you were looking for. Her whole *modus operandi* involved using a honeypot or a honey-trap. Once you went for the "honey," she had you trapped. And when she had you, the extortion came next; and if you didn't want your dirty little secrets, kinks, or perversions exposed, you paid up. If you were lucky, you paid a one-time fee. If not, your long-term payout could last for months, years . . . or indefinitely.

HOMER

Did she only extort the marks for money?

MUSE

Sometimes she was looking for financial payouts, and sometimes for information. Helen would also broker the info in addition to the extortion. Why just collect blackmail proceeds when you can also make money by selling the mark's information to the highest bidder?

HOMER

She was compensated from both ends. Cash from the mark being blackmailed, and cash from those who would profit from the mark's shame and downfall.

MUSE

You got it. On paper, the plan is a win-win for Helen. But in reality, it's a fifty-fifty split because the scam can only be run on select people.

HOMER

How so?

MUSE

Imagine some dude, or dudette, gets caught with their pants down or skirt up—literally and figuratively. Helen compromises and blackmails them. They have to pay up or the compromising information goes public. With me so far?

HOMER

Yeah. I'm with you. Continue.

MUSE

Okay, the compromised person starts paying the blackmail, so no one finds out. Everything's good, right?

HOMER

Yeah, assuming you can trust that the blackmailer won't just take the payout and expose you anyway.

MUSE

Sure, but as long as the payouts keep coming in, Helen should have no reason to make the information public, right?

HOMER

Agreed.

MUSE

Now let's say our compromised person is an industry mogul or some other type of bigwig. It's a sure bet that a high-ranking person has rivals looking to gain any kind of advantage. Let's say the compromised person shares inside information or industry secrets during pillow talk with Helen or an operative. The target's trying to show how powerful, smart, and important he is. If you're Helen, what's the next logical step?

HOMER

She, or one of her operatives, now possesses information that can be sold to the compromised person's rival—information that could ruin the mark publicly, personally, professionally, and quite possibly financially.

MUSE

Bingo. But that plan has an inherent flaw. This tactic is a one-time play. If the information is sold to a third party, then the mark can no longer pay blackmail because he just lost everything. And the information sold to the mark's rival may only be viable, or valuable, to that one particular person and for one particular instance.

HOMER

So, the goose that lays the golden egg is essentially killed?

MUSE

Exactly. And now Helen has to move to the next mark. Granted, marks are in no short supply, but scouting is work, and you don't always get a high return on your investment. Helen became a master at running these ops on athletes, celebs, et cetera. But these people have a shelf life. Once a celeb is no longer in the spotlight or relevant, he becomes washed-up and basically worthless. The long game is in business and politics.

HOMER
Why those two fields?

MUSE
Because these people tend to have longevity. They're fed information every day throughout their careers or terms in office. Helen essentially turned them in the same way a case officer spots, recruits, and turns a spy. The info flows in, and the blackmail and hush money flows out. Plus, there's an added bonus.

HOMER
What's that?

MUSE
Helen now has information that can be sold, traded, stored away for a rainy day, or used.

HOMER
Used, how?

MUSE
Business and politics go hand in hand, right?

HOMER
Right.

MUSE
Think stocks, trading, investing.

HOMER
Understood. Go on.

MUSE

Ever notice how some politicians come into office not having been fabulously wealthy; but somehow, they become rich while they're in office or leave office miraculously wealthy?

HOMER

Yeah.

MUSE

I can't wrap my head around how they suddenly get lucky with finances and become extremely savvy investors overnight.

HOMER

That's a no-brainer. They get fed insider information in exchange for political favors.

MUSE

I was being sarcastic but thank you for making my point. Helen tapped into this well-known truth, and by going after politicians and high-level business executives, she could keep bleeding them dry until there was nothing worthwhile left.

HOMER

I sense a *but* coming here.

MUSE

The *but* was in picking the right target. She needed long-serving targets, people entrenched in their positions. She needed these people to be overly ambitious, easy to control, and not as bright as they thought they were.

HOMER

But you said earlier that she, and her organization, mostly dealt

with state-level politicians, state reps, and state assembly people . . . maybe a governor.

MUSE

She also started to branch out to national-level politicians. If rumor can be believed, she had a couple of big-city mayors in her
pocket, too.

HOMER

So, I return to my earlier question: why Zeus?

MUSE

Why not? Everyone knows that the guy can't keep it in his pants,
and he's a braggart and a blabbermouth on top of that.

HOMER

That braggart and blabbermouth does rule from Olympus.

MUSE

So what? I didn't vote for the fucking guy, and I don't like
him, either.

HOMER

But you're not above taking his money. I've seen your books.
You've collected on several contracts that came directly
from Olympus.

MUSE

Again, so what? I'm good at my job, and if you're good at something, you never do it for free. I provide a service. Zeus contracted for my services. I completed those contracts and was paid
for them. I don't have to like someone to take his money. And
I certainly don't have to swear some undying blood oath to that

person before I'm compensated. Do you mean to tell me that you've liked every single boss you've ever worked for?

HOMER

Of course not, but what I'm trying to figure out is how Helen even met Zeus, let alone got close to him.

MUSE

How do rich, powerful, and beautiful people usually meet?

HOMER

That's what I'm trying to piece together.

MUSE

The question was rhetorical. They met each other doing rich, powerful, and beautiful people shit like attending galas, fundraisers, awards shows, and major sporting events. Here, all those lower-level politicians, lobbyists, and businesspeople come into play. Any one of them could have set up a meet and greet, or whatever. The bottom line is that Zeus and Helen did meet; the rest, as they say, is history.

HOMER

Or infamy.

MUSE

Preach, brother.

HOMER

First off, I'm not your brother. Second, before we get any deeper in the weeds on this subject, I want to know what you have on Helen. What do you know?

MUSE

Me? What do I have on Helen? What do I know about her? What kind of bullshit debrief is this? You folks recruited her, trained her, and made her who she was . . . not me.

HOMER

You've got the wrong three-letter agency, and that place isn't exactly forthcoming with her origin story. Look, I'm recreating the wheel here. I'm building my file from scratch. This is where you come in. And you're right about something you said before.

MUSE

What's that?

HOMER

You are good. You know things I don't. By helping me, you're really helping yourself. You're smart, too. You know that cooperating is your only real play, at least if you want to try and salvage what's left of your company and career. So, I'll ask you again. What else can you tell me about Helen?

SECTION 3

MUSE

I'm sure you guys have already done your initial background on her—open-source searches, public records, all that. I'll try to fill in some of the lesser-known details.

HOMER

Such as?

MUSE

Helen Argos, as you may or may not know, was the daughter of Leda Argos.

HOMER

The supermodel?

MUSE

The same. And by all accounts, Helen lived a charmed life—the best schools, the best teachers, the best clothes. She wanted for nothing and had everything. After university, she worked at her mother's modeling agency, Swan. And not surprisingly, she became just as famous, if not more famous, than her mom. Helen has been called "The Most Beautiful Woman in the World," and once her career took off, no doors were closed to her. She had money, power, and most importantly, access to people who were equally powerful and famous. Whether by plan or coincidence, a certain espionage-focused governmental agency came calling and recruited her into Project Vixen.

HOMER

What's Project Vixen? Is it similar to the Lioness Program the military ran?

MUSE

No. The Lioness Program was a boots-on-the-ground, tactical-level, hearts-and-minds type of program. Vixen was altogether different. The only thing the two programs have in common is that women are the primary operators.

HOMER

Interesting. So, what do you know about Vixen?

MUSE

Vixen was modeled after the Sparrows Program. But unlike the Sparrows, who went after anyone they thought could be of value, the Vixens only went after the big fish. Their targets include top-level cultural, political, military, and industry people worldwide. Because the Vixens held a high-level status of their own, they could essentially go anywhere, do anything, and get next to whoever they wanted.

HOMER

Hiding in plain sight?

MUSE

Exactly. No one suspects that the insanely beautiful person chatting them up is up to no good. That's the basic premise behind Vixen.

HOMER

Okay. What else do you know?

MUSE

Helen was recruited and went through training. But this training didn't include your typical spy school stuff like throat-cutting
and bomb-throwing. Helen was taught how to extract a target's
deepest, darkest secrets. Targets think they're giving up these secrets of their own free will—that's how good the school is.

HOMER

So why would she go to work for the government? She certainly
didn't need the money.

MUSE

No. She did not.

HOMER

You mentioned two versions of an acronym earlier—an acronym
of vices. What drives a person. Doesn't that work both ways?

MUSE

What do you mean?

HOMER

Helen wasn't motivated by money, so there goes the *M*. She didn't
appear to be motivated by the thought, prospect, or even possibility of getting to have sex with the targets, so there goes the *S*.
She wasn't compromised, so there goes the *C*, if we're using the
other variation of the acronym. That leaves the *I* for ideology and
the *E* for ego. So, was it pride motivating her all this time?

MUSE

No, she was motivated by something entirely outside any acronym. She wanted revenge.

SECTION 4

HOMER

Revenge? For what?

MUSE

I have a theory, but let's go through your train of thought—it connects the pieces and brings everything together.

HOMER

Okay.

MUSE

Helen was in high demand because of her position and status within Swan. She was a model with the ability—and legitimate justification—to travel anywhere in the world for any number of purposes, like photo shoots, fashion shows, charity events, humanitarian projects, or any public event. Would you agree?

HOMER

Sure, I agree.

MUSE

Helen knew that the government wanted to use her, so she used them to teach her things that she couldn't learn on her own. You following so far?

HOMER

I am.

MUSE

In the eyes of the government, she already had a perfect, legitimate cover that didn't need to be created or backstopped. Her situation was a match made in espionage heaven. Both sides were using each other without either side knowing. Here is where my theory comes into play. What the government didn't know was that Helen used her training to form her proof of concept for a future endeavor upon her separation from service.

HOMER

And what was that endeavor?

MUSE

She planned to run her own Vixen-style operation for personal gain.

HOMER

So, Helen was ego-driven? She thought she could run a private intelligence program better than the government?

MUSE

Close, but not quite.

HOMER

Well, her motive couldn't have been ideologically based because we have no confirmed instances of her being politically or religiously motivated. So, I keep coming back to the question—what was her drive?

MUSE

As I said earlier, revenge. That one intangible that can't be influenced by money, sex, ideology, or ego.

HOMER

Okay, I'm inclined to agree with you, but what was she seeking revenge against?

MUSE

This is the key part of my theory. She sought revenge not against *what* but against *who*. And I believe that who is Zeus. And not for the position Zeus holds, or what that position represents, but revenge on Zeus as a person, as a targeted individual.

HOMER

Why?

MUSE

This part of my theory has been kicking around in the back of my mind since the whole thing started.

HOMER

Which is?

MUSE

By all accounts, Helen served her time in government service admirably and honorably. Rumor is that she retired after a full career and even collected a pension.

HOMER

For real?

MUSE

That's what I heard. I also heard that after government service, she went back to Swan to run the company as its chief executive officer. Her mother died and left her the business, and then Helen implemented her plan. She established a private, off-the-books version of Vixen, and the government she once served was none the wiser. Timing's everything, right?

HOMER

Yeah. I guess.

MUSE

These events nicely coincide with the time Helen starts orbiting Zeus.

HOMER

Go on.

MUSE

Have you ever heard the phrase "history repeats itself"?

HOMER

Of course I have. But what history did Helen and Zeus have? Prior to this incident, we have zero intelligence to indicate that the two even met, let alone existed in the same zip code.

MUSE

Here's the biggest part of my theory, and please keep in mind that this is all rumor intelligence. But plenty of folks in the private intelligence world have all told each other this same campfire story.

HOMER

And what would that story be?

MUSE

That Zeus was Helen's biological father.

SECTION 5

HOMER

What!?

MUSE

Pretty wild, right? But think about it. The story makes sense. Zeus is a well-known philanderer, and it's an open secret that he fathered many children—from many different women—outside of wedlock. The guy's been around for a long time. A leopard can't change its spots. He was a horny young man, so is it really a stretch to assume that he's now a horny old man?

HOMER

Okay, he's a horny guy. So what? It still doesn't connect Helen to Zeus. You seem to be shaping a backstory to match the current narrative. It's all speculation.

MUSE

Fair enough. I see where you're coming from but try this next part on for size: Zeus was rumored to have had an affair with Leda Argos.

HOMER

Helen's mother? How long ago?

MUSE

About forty-five years ago.

HOMER

And how old is Helen?

MUSE

About forty-five.

HOMER

Son of a bitch! Wait; you aren't saying that Zeus met Helen later in life and had sex with his own daughter . . . are you?

MUSE

No. But according to my sources, he tried.

HOMER

That is deeply disturbing and disgustingly illegal.

MUSE

To be fair, he likely doesn't know that he knocked up Leda Argos. Not that any foreknowledge takes away from the creepiness of the whole thing, but I don't believe that Zeus would knowingly commit incest. I think he just thought that Helen was another woman he could seduce, and Helen strung him along. Do you remember trying to chase that hot chick in high school or college? Everyone's got one of those.

HOMER

Unfortunately, I can relate.

MUSE

Remember how you would say or do anything just to get close to her? Nothing would ever happen, but you'd keep playing the game because she'd always keep that hope alive?

HOMER

Yeah, but what's that got to do with Helen and Zeus?

MUSE

Because Helen did the same thing here. She got Zeus to say things that he shouldn't have, got him to do things that he shouldn't do, just to impress a woman who never had any intention of consummating the relationship. She played the long game on Zeus. She collected every scrap of gossip, information, or intel that she could get out of him and then dropped a bomb on him.

HOMER

The "I am your daughter" bomb?

MUSE

That's the one. I theorize that this is how her plan started to take shape. She figured she'd blackmail Zeus, and if he didn't play ball, she'd go public with the fact that he not only had an affair with Leda Argos but also got her pregnant and left her to raise the child on her own. Trying to seduce and sleep with his own offspring would be the sadistic cherry on top.

HOMER

If that ever went public, Zeus wouldn't be forgiven. Incest is a line no society will cross.

MUSE

Exactly. But the *coup de grace* for Helen was that even when Zeus started paying her hush money, Helen still sold all her intel to Hera.

HOMER

Hera? As in the First Lady of Olympus?

MUSE

Yeah, Zeus' wife, but also his main political rival. It's well-known that their marriage is nothing but window dressing to keep up appearances for the good of the nation. She has her eyes on the throne, and armed with this information, she could take Zeus off the board and find herself running the government from Olympus. Hera was aware of all the times Zeus stepped out on her. But she put up with all the infidelity because as he rose in power, she did too. But the situation with Helen was the proverbial straw that broke the camel's back, and if she didn't strike while the iron was hot, *both* Hera and Zeus would be ruined.

HOMER

From what you're telling me, Zeus was caught between a rock and a hard place—Helen being the rock and Hera the hard place.

MUSE

Yeah, he was caught in a classic pincer movement, of sorts.

HOMER

I'm starting to think that your theory holds weight. So, did Zeus decide to take direct action against Helen around this time?

MUSE

Yes. At first, he ordered Hermes , the director of national intelligence, to . . . let's just say . . . *kinetically* solve the problem. Hermes told Zeus that he couldn't do that. Zeus wanted to know why the fuck not. Hermes then divulged two pieces of information. First, Helen was a citizen, and as such, he could not legally target and kill her. And second, Helen was a retired intelligence operative.

HOMER

What did Zeus do with this information?

MUSE

Zeus decided to go black, and I mean deep black. He ordered a completely off-the-books contract to be put out to the two biggest companies in the private military contracting and private intelligence world, Hoplite and Trojan. The contract was simple—capture or kill Helen Argos.

ATTACHMENT 1

CASE NOTES: PRIVATE MILITARY AND INTELLIGENCE CONTRACTING COMPANIES

- Private military and intelligence contractors provide armed direct action services and/or security (physical and cyber) services. They furthermore offer intelligence-gathering and analytic services.

- The services offered by these private companies are similar to those usually provided by governments.

- These private companies also provide training and instruction to governmental agencies in various disciplines.

- Another function these companies perform is close protection work (also known as bodyguarding) of not only government officials but also wealthy private citizens who desire protection from threats, real or imagined.

- According to a recent study conducted by national intelligence resources, private military and intelligence contractors make up approximately 30 percent of the intelligence community's workforce and cost roughly the equivalent of 50 percent of their total personnel budgets.

- Private contractors who engage in armed combat in a declared war zone may be considered "unlawful combatants" according to the international laws of armed conflict.

SECTION 6

MUSE

At this point, Helen is no longer the focal point. She becomes a background presence, like a river that continuously flows and carries everyone along with it. Essentially, she was the justification for what happened next. From now on, when you think of Helen, think of her as "the face that launched a thousand drones."

HOMER

So, what are the focal points then?

MUSE

What I want to focus on first is Hoplite and its four founding members: Agamemnon, Agamemnon's brother, Menalaus, Nestor, and Priam.

HOMER

Hold on. Why aren't we still focused on Helen?

MUSE

Because she's a moot point. You already know how this whole thing ended. We have to get into the other players in this game.

HOMER

Why?

MUSE

Because these are the people who directly shaped the following events. We'll get back to Helen, but first, let's talk about these guys. What do you know about them?

HOMER

Only what's open-source. They've been written about online and in trade publications. I've been to a few training courses run by Hoplite and Trojan. Good classes. The instructors were top-notch, but I don't know much about the people at the top. That's another reason you're here—to provide situational knowledge, institutional knowledge, and industry knowledge.

MUSE

Well, one thing that's not widely known outside of military and intelligence circles is that Agamemnon, Menalaus, Nestor, and Priam all knew one another before pursuing the private contracting world.

HOMER

Can you expound?

MUSE

Sure. They all grew up together. They played on the same sports teams. They went to the same schools. And then they all enlisted in the military together.

HOMER

What branch?

MUSE

Army. They became paratroopers. They all attended the same one-unit station for basic training, infantry school, and jump school. Then they all went to the same airborne unit and deployed together on combat operations around the world. From there, they pursued and passed a selection course for entry into an elite special operations light infantry regiment. But here is where their paths started to diverge.

HOMER

In what way?

MUSE

Agamemnon went into a special forces operational detachment; Menalaus stayed with the elite light infantry regiment; Nestor went into a civil affairs unit; and Priam went to a psychological operations team.

HOMER

Okay. What else can you tell me?

MUSE

According to people who served with them, and any evaluations or fitness reports I could get my hands on, they served brilliantly at each of their respective commands. They even came back together again when they successfully screened for a special missions unit, a unit where they served out the rest of their careers. At this special missions unit, rumor has it that they formed the idea of starting their own private contracting company when they got out. This was the genesis of what became Aegis.

HOMER

Aegis? Didn't that company go bankrupt? And what does Aegis have to do with Hoplite and Trojan?

MUSE

Hoplite and Trojan were originally one entity named Aegis. And yeah, that company went tits up. You want my opinion as to why?

HOMER

That's why you're here and why I'm talking to you.

MUSE

Aegis failed because Agamemnon is a fucking prick.

HOMER

Come on, tell me something I don't know. Agamemnon being a prick is as well-known as Zeus' extramarital activities.

MUSE

You're missing my point. Aegis failed because the four of them couldn't operate in an environment that wasn't already set up and designed to function in a top-down hierarchical manner.

HOMER

But these guys grew up together, played sports together, and served together. Now, after all these years, they suddenly couldn't work together? That doesn't make sense.

MUSE

You're right, it doesn't make sense, but the activities you listed all have one thing in common.

HOMER

Which is?

MUSE

Structure. Sports have rules, boundaries, referees, and umpires that monitor what you can and can't do. Teams have coaches, trainers, and practices. They weren't exactly playing pick-up ball, and even then, the rules of that game are known and understood.

HOMER

I think I know where you're going. Continue.

MUSE

In the military, similar to sports teams, there's a chain of command. There are junior and senior enlisted, junior and senior non-commissioned officers, and junior and senior officers. There are tactics, techniques, and procedures for everything. There's even doctrine, a way to do everything from the individual level to the group level, from the tactical level to the operational and strategic level.

HOMER

Okay, I understand what you're saying, but I still don't see why Aegis failed.

MUSE

Contracting is the private sector, and no massive bureaucracy dictates or tells you what needs to be done or how. Taxpayer money no longer funds operations.

HOMER

But wouldn't their work be like your pick-up ball analogy? Contracting is basically the same job they were doing in the military, right?

MUSE

It's an oversimplification, but yes. Look at the situation this way—pick-up ball only works short-term and only as long as all the players agree to follow all the rules. No one can try to change or interpret the rules as they see fit. Even worse would be a player who doesn't abide by rules, penalties, or fouls at all—or does so selectively. Basically, at the end of the day, you can play a pick-up game, but not a pick-up season. Aegis tried the season.

HOMER

I'm starting to follow; can you explain further?

MUSE

The first few contracts went well because they were small, manageable contracts. But as time progressed, the contracts that Aegis worked on became more complex.

HOMER

And, let me guess. This pick-up ball mentality started to backfire because Aegis was like a sandlot team going up against a professional team?

MUSE

Exactly, and these complex operations put a strain on the personal and professional relationships of these four men. What people forget, or don't know, about military or government service of any kind is that these organizations have a budget paid for by the taxpayer. So even if something fails spectacularly, the government loses no money. But people working in the private sector put their personal money on the line, so failing can mean the difference between keeping the doors open and the lights on or closing up shop for good.

HOMER

Okay, now I'm following you. These guys now had to worry about things that they never had to worry about in their old line of work, correct?

MUSE

Yeah. Here's another thought exercise. Say you get a million dollars for a contract. That million gets split four ways—two hundred and fifty thousand each. Not bad, right?

HOMER

Sounds pretty good to me.

MUSE

But along comes our friend, *expenses.* Most people only think about the money that a contractor makes as an individual, and Agamemnon, Menalaus, Nestor, and Priam were all still in government service during the golden age of contracting when these companies and the individual contractors were pulling in record numbers and profits. But those numbers only accounted for "front of the house" type of stuff. What about the "back of the house"?

HOMER

What about it? You're starting to lose me again.

MUSE

Okay, your agency-issued vehicle breaks down. What do you do?

HOMER

I bring the vehicle to fleet maintenance.

MUSE

How much of that maintenance fee comes out of your own pocket?

HOMER

None. It's budgeted for.

MUSE

How about when you go to the range? Do you buy your own guns?

HOMER

No.

MUSE

How about ammo? Do you buy your own?

HOMER

No.

MUSE

How about equipment? Uniforms? Boots? Body armor? Do you buy any of those things with your own money?

HOMER

No. They're all issued to me.

MUSE

Right. Now let's expand beyond individual expenses. Are you responsible for payroll? Insurance? Property management? Building maintenance? Office supplies or office equipment acquisition?

HOMER

No, human resources and the office managers handle all that.

MUSE

Are you responsible for funding your own pension for retirement?

HOMER

No. I get it. It's the behind-the-scenes stuff that no one thinks about that makes a whole organization work, and having to fund all the administrative and support elements really started to cut into that two hundred and fifty thousand that Agamemnon and the others got.

MUSE

Exactly. And here's one of the cons of private contracting. The military, law enforcement, fire department, and emergency medical services can more or less accurately predict how many people will separate from service each year. So, they also have a rough estimate of how many employees they'll need to replace those going out. If all goes well, they wind up with a net gain.

HOMER

But contracting doesn't work this way?

MUSE

Hell no. You never know how many contracts a person has left in him.

HOMER

You don't? Why not?

MUSE

Mileage on the body. Wear and tear. Not all, but most contractors come into the industry after serving a whole career elsewhere. Those twenty-plus years of experience come with all the injuries, aches, and pains from that previous job. Bad backs, shoulders, knees, et cetera. With me so far?

HOMER

I am. Go on.

MUSE

Of course, a seasoned contractor walks in the door with all the training and experience from that career. That's definitely a pro. But at the end of the day, the physical and mental toll from that previous life can act like a ticking time bomb, waiting to detonate and derail a contract at any moment. It can happen right out of the gate.

HOMER

Okay, so what you're saying is that a contractor may work multiple contracts for years or they may not even complete one. I hadn't considered that contractors could be an unreliable investment. I had this completely different picture in my mind.

MUSE

Most people do. People also don't consider that when a firm holds screenings or tryouts, the company doesn't really know who's going to show up.

HOMER

What do you mean?

MUSE

The guy or gal applying may look great on paper, but that ideal person might not be who shows up on test day. Someone could show up who can no longer shoot accurately, isn't safe on the range, can't pass the run, or can't meet the push-up and sit-up requirements—and that's just the physical qualifications.

HOMER

What about the mental?

MUSE

I was getting there. Imagine that this candidate crushes the physical fitness test but can't pass the psychological or written aptitude tests—or can't stay sober long enough to even show up for a screening.

HOMER

I can see how that would be a problem.

MUSE

If the company's lucky, these people can pull their heads out of their asses and get their shit together. But it usually doesn't work out that way.

HOMER

So ultimately, the company winds up losing more people than it's able to bring in?

MUSE

Correct. And that, plus all the behind-the-scenes costs, is what Aegis was up against as it started to grow. It's what all contracting firms are up against all the time.

HOMER

Again, it's something I never even considered. I had this preconceived notion in my head about private military contractors.

MUSE

There's another way to look at the company-contractor relationship. On one hand, the company has no long-term investment in the contractor because some other employer has already made that initial investment. On the other hand, you might wind up with someone else's damaged goods because you didn't make that initial long-term investment in recruiting, training, supervision, and retention. Get it?

HOMER

I do.

MUSE

This very issue is why Agamemnon and Priam had a falling out.

HOMER

What you're saying is all very interesting, but what do the every-day problems of the private contracting world have to do with Operation Trojan War?

MUSE

I'm getting to my point. Please be patient. You need the backstory so that when you look at what transpired later, everything makes sense. Nothing happens in a vacuum.

HOMER

Fair enough. Please continue.

MUSE

Agamemnon wanted to run things the traditional way. Bid on a contract, accept the contract, host screenings to fill out the personnel roster, work that contract. Rinse and repeat.

HOMER

What was his thought process?

MUSE

He thought that he could always find someone to fill a spot, that the former action guys and girls were always looking for work. Plus, he didn't have to spend a dime of his own money to train them. To him, this method translated to more money in his pocket. Technically, he was right.

HOMER

And what was Priam's thought process?

MUSE

Priam wanted to shift the paradigm and develop personnel from the ground up. Those under him would be fully indoctrinated into the "contractor way of life" and wouldn't come into the field with expectations on how things should be done.

HOMER

So, Priam wanted employees, not hired guns?

MUSE

Correct. Priam wanted employees, and he wanted those employees to be one hundred percent loyal to the company—not to the highest bidder with the deepest pockets. He wanted people for the long term, not people looking for a quick payday. Ultimately, he wanted to take the mercenary aspect out of contracting to professionalize and legitimize the industry.

HOMER

Okay. I'm tracking with what you're saying, but the logical question becomes *who*, right? Who is chosen to be part of that first recruit class? You can't just pick some random person off the street because they might not be cut out for contracting. Even someone who might work well at a contracting firm, like in support or admin, wouldn't necessarily work in-theater.

MUSE

Exactly. But Priam's plan accounted for that too. He wanted to recruit and train people to fill specific roles within the company that best suited them. He wanted everyone to initially go through a basic training program so there would be commonality of training. If a member of the support or administrative staff ever found themselves in a tactical situation, they would at least have some knowledge of what to do. Priam's plan was a long-term play that would take time and money to fully implement.

HOMER

Agreed.

MUSE

But Priam's immediate concern in proving that his concept of operation would work was filling the role most commonly associated with a high-end private military contracting company.

HOMER

What was that role?

MUSE

The door kicker, the trigger puller, and the pipe hitter roles.

HOMER

Did he have anyone in mind?

MUSE

Priam already had two test subjects ready to go. His thinking was that if he could train these two men from the ground up, then his concept would work going forward.

HOMER

Who were the two candidates?

MUSE

His two sons. Hector and Paris.

SECTION 7

HOMER

What was Priam's time frame for training?

MUSE

A one-to-two-year pipeline.

HOMER

And what would that period entail?

MUSE

Basic training followed by advanced individual training and specialized courses like jump school and free fall school. Candidates would then move on to a special operations type selection and assessment course. This would be enough to get them to an operational level in the team. Once employees reached this stage, they underwent specific qualification training to develop proficiency in essential core tasks.

HOMER

You mentioned getting employees to operational elements. Would they be integrated into existing teams of contractors? I thought Priam wanted to do away with the contracting model and replace the cut-and-dried template with his vision?

MUSE

He did, but that vision would take time. You can't throw the baby out with the bathwater, and to be honest, you can't completely move away from having contractors. Priam figured by the time all was said and done, he'd be looking at a two-to-four-year training and work-up period so that by year five, the candidates would be fully up to speed and able to operate with their element.

HOMER

What about the projected cost of running this program?

MUSE

Priam had a brilliant workaround. His plan was to take a step back from operational contracts and focus on training contracts. That way, he'd be able to keep bringing money into Aegis while providing Hector and Paris with the training they needed.

HOMER

And how was that plan received by Agamemnon?

MUSE

His answer was a hard no.

HOMER

Why the vitriol? This seems like a solid, common-sense approach, and a well-thought-out, long-term plan like that would provide stability and longevity to the company.

MUSE

You would think so, but Agamemnon took Priam's proposal as a personal insult and threat, both personally and professionally.

HOMER

How so?

MUSE

Because, in the not-so-distant future, Hector and Paris would be fully up to speed, running operational elements and overseeing contracts themselves. Then it would only be a matter of time before Priam, Hector, and Paris would outnumber Agamemnon on the board of directors.

HOMER

So, in Agamemnon's mind, he'd get voted out and Priam and his sons would take over Aegis?

MUSE

Correct.

HOMER

And that wasn't Priam's plan?

MUSE

No. Priam was a true believer. He believed in his role within the military and his work with Aegis. He believed his new plan would fill a necessary gap in the market. But more importantly, he believed that this was *a way* and not necessarily *the way* . . . which is to say, Agamemnon's way.

HOMER

What happened?

MUSE

Because he believed in his plan, Priam forced a vote of the Aegis board of directors.

HOMER

How did the voting breakdown?

MUSE

Pretty much along party lines.

HOMER

Can you elaborate?

MUSE

Agamemnon was a no. Priam was a yes. Menalaus backed his brother's play and voted no. That left Nestor. If he voted no, the matter would be dead in the water. If he voted yes, the vote would be tied, but in the event of a tie vote, Agamemnon, as the senior founding member, could break the tie and decide the matter.

HOMER

So how did Nestor vote?

MUSE

He abstained, citing a conflict of interest. He felt he couldn't be truly neutral and detached.

HOMER

So, the final tally was two in opposition against one in favor with one abstaining?

MUSE

Correct. Priam's plan was voted down.

HOMER

What happened after the vote?

MUSE

Priam tendered his resignation from Aegis on the spot. His plan was his legacy. He felt that the company should be left to their children so that they could continue to build what their fathers created. His plan was a plan of succession. At its core, it was a long-term continuity of operations plan. But there was no way Agamemnon would let Priam's plan happen.

HOMER

Was this done out of spite?

MUSE

More like a mix of spite with a dash of righteous indignation. Agamemnon didn't really care what happened to Aegis after he retired or died. His way of thinking was that he served his country and then served himself, getting rich along the way. Why should he leave his company to some ungrateful offspring to squander away his life's work? If his children wanted something, then they would have to go out and work for it. When privately asked about the falling out with Priam, he is rumored to have said, "Fuck him and fuck his kids, too." Agamemnon only thought of himself and of personal gain. Other people were a means used to achieve this end.

HOMER

Did Agamemnon let Priam walk?

MUSE

No. A short legal battle took place after Priam resigned.

HOMER

What was the outcome?

MUSE

A judge ultimately ruled in Priam's favor saying that any non-disclosure agreements or non-compete agreements that Priam previously signed were null and void. The judge also ordered that Agamemnon, Menalaus, and Nestor buy out the twenty-five percent of the company shares that Priam owned, a purchase that effectively broke the financial back of Aegis. The company continued to exist, but only on paper. Aegis ceased all operations and eventually dissolved as an entity. The company would later be resurrected as Hoplite. The rivalry between Agamemnon and Priam officially began.

SECTION 8

HOMER

So Aegis, previously one company, split and became two companies?

MUSE

Not exactly. Let me explain, because what came next was truly groundbreaking and revolutionary for our industry in one aspect, but in another aspect, it was pretty status quo.

HOMER

Okay, what was so groundbreaking?

MUSE

Trojan was one entity. One company. Priam executed his plan when he left Aegis and started operations with Trojan. He took his buyout money and used it to construct a state-of-the-art training and headquarters facility. He began teaching all kinds of courses to ex-military personnel, law enforcement officers, and even civilians. And, true to his word, he enrolled Hector and Paris in these courses to build their foundational skills. Within a few years, his sons were teaching courses, overseeing programs, and planning their own training operations.

HOMER

So, Trojan was a training company at the beginning?

MUSE

Yeah, that's how it started out. And as the training side of the house grew, Priam began accepting not only domestic training contracts throughout the country but international training contracts as well.

HOMER

Who did Trojan cater to?

MUSE

Domestically, Trojan focused on local, county, state, and federal law enforcement and offered conventional patrol tactics along with special weapons and tactics teams. Trojan also began picking up special operations military contracts in-country and internationally. Priam sent Hector and Paris across the world to equip them with advanced skill sets. At this point, and on paper, Hector and Paris were the equivalent of their peers in military special operations forces, at least on the white side.

HOMER

What's the white side?

MUSE

Non-tier-one elements or non-special mission units. But, for Priam's plan to be truly successful, his sons needed the real-world experience that Priam himself received while serving in the military with Agamemnon, Menalaus, and Nestor. Fortunately, Priam had a back door that would put his sons into an element comparable to the military tier-one and special mission units.

HOMER

And what was that back door?

MUSE

Priam knew a certain intelligence agency staffed with paramilitary officers who served in a global response capacity.

HOMER

Could you define *global response capacity*?

MUSE

Its officers engage in operations around the world under the director of that particular agency. The members of this global response staff are called special agents and spend significant portions of their time deployed abroad. These agents support operations as team leaders and project managers . . . shit like that.

HOMER

How did Hector and Paris qualify to get it? What are the standards?

MUSE

Funny enough, for all the secret squirrel stuff that people think goes on, the standards are listed right on their website. It's open-source information.

HOMER

Really?

MUSE

Yeah, really. Weird, huh? Anyway, here are the standards: a high school diploma or GED and extensive military, intelligence, or law enforcement experience. Obviously, preferred candidates come from a military special operations unit, but this agency will take you if you have experience as a law enforcement special weapons and tactics officer or as an undercover officer. Hell, if you have experience in executive protection, they'll take you. Additionally, you need to be physically, medically, and emotionally fit. You need excellent written and oral communication skills and analytical skills. You need to play well with others, have good conflict resolution and organizational skills, and display flexibility and adaptability.

HOMER

Anything else?

MUSE

You need to demonstrate leadership and supervisory abilities and be able to interact with all levels of management. You have to be loyal, honest, and trustworthy. Finally, you have to be willing to work in some of the most dangerous places in the world. Shitholes, to be blunt.

HOMER

And Hector and Paris checked off all of these boxes?

MUSE

They'd been to war zones—albeit in an instructor capacity, but they'd been there. They had the training and experience in tactical and protection operations. They had supervisory and managerial experience. They had the tactical medical training, and they could do the administrative portion of the job as well. So yeah, I'd say they checked all the boxes.

HOMER

But you said it yourself. Their training and experience was from the instructor side and not from the end-user side.

MUSE

True. Priam being their father certainly greased the wheels and didn't hurt their chances of being selected. But they would have been selected regardless.

HOMER

Why?

MUSE

Because they're just that good.

HOMER

What time frame are we looking at here while all this is going on?

MUSE

Probably around the seven-year mark of Trojan's founding. Since getting the company fully running would take about a year, I figure Hector and Paris had been at work for about six years.

HOMER

And this timetable was in line with Priam's vision?

MUSE

Yeah, it's about a one-to-two-year pipeline just to make it to an operational element. Then it's probably about another three to four years to get up to speed on core competencies and mission-essential tasks. Trojan was right on track.

HOMER

So, Priam's plan worked? He was able to prove his concept?

MUSE

I'd say so.

HOMER

How long did Hector and Paris operate as paramilitary special agents with that global response group?

MUSE

Ten years. Hector was twenty-two when he entered Priam's training pipeline. At year six, he got picked up by that global response group, so he was about twenty-eight at that point. He worked ten years with the global response group and then returned to Trojan when he was about thirty-eight.

HOMER

What about Paris?

MUSE

He was younger. He entered Priam's training pipeline at eighteen, so at year six, he was twenty-four. He spent ten years with that global response group right alongside his brother. They both left at the ten-year mark to go back to Trojan, so Paris would have been about thirty-four at the time.

HOMER

And what happened when Priam reunited with his sons?

MUSE

Trojan took off and started dominating the private contracting world.

SECTION 9

HOMER

So, what was happening with Agamemnon during this timeframe?

MUSE

After Aegis dissolved and the lawsuit was settled, Agamemnon, Menalaus, and Nestor were able to raise enough capital to start their new contracting company, Hoplite.

HOMER

You mentioned that Hoplite was different than Trojan. Can you explain how?

MUSE

At first, Agamemnon ran Hoplite like he did Aegis. And at first, this model worked—Priam was building his company and his training facility and headquarters space, so Hoplite was off and running because it didn't have to compete with Trojan for contracts. When Trojan became fully operational and started focusing on training and instructing contracts, Hoplite felt a cut in its market share. However, Hoplite was able to offset the competition because, at that time, Trojan wasn't taking real-world operational contracting gigs. And while Hector and Paris were off with the global response group doing their postgraduate studies—a.k.a gaining real-world training and experience—Trojan still only focused on the training and instructing side of contracting while Hoplite focused on the operational side.

HOMER

Seems like a pretty tenuous balance between the two companies.

MUSE

It was. The two companies had a "you don't fuck with me, and I won't fuck with you, and we'll both be okay" type of agreement.

HOMER

And how long did this homeostasis last?

MUSE

Right up until Hector and Paris left the global response group and returned to Trojan. At this point, Trojan started winning bids for both training *and* operational contracts.

HOMER

So, at this point, Trojan became a direct threat to Hoplite, correct?

MUSE

Correct. Agamemnon realized that he had to find a different way to operate if he wanted his company to survive.

HOMER

So, what did he do? How did he make Hoplite different from Trojan?

MUSE

Remember when I said that Agamemnon was a fucking prick?

HOMER

Yes.

MUSE

Well, I should have added that he's a smart fucking prick.

Arrogant, too. But he's got a brilliant mind for both war fighting and business. He read the tea leaves and knew Priam and Trojan were on to something. As much as he hated to admit it, he also knew Priam's concept worked. Now, he would *never* publicly admit that fact or adopt Priam's model, because that's just not him. Agamemnon would never give Priam the satisfaction of being able to say, "I told you so."

HOMER

Again, what did he do? How did Agamemnon respond?

MUSE

This is where Agamemnon comes up with his own concept of operations.

HOMER

Which was?

MUSE

If Priam was going to recruit, train, and retain from the ground up, then Agamemnon would use an affiliation model.

HOMER

Affiliation? Like a franchise?

MUSE

No. In its own way, this move was totally different and radical for our industry.

HOMER

How so?

MUSE

Franchises are run exactly the same way, right?

HOMER

Right.

MUSE

You walk into any major fast-food chain, and they all kinda look the same—laid out the same, staffed, and run the same. Uniforms, menus, all the same. You know exactly what you're getting when you go to one of these places. No surprises. Affiliations are different.

HOMER

How?

MUSE

Agamemnon looked to a well-known functional fitness company and took a page right out of its playbook.

HOMER

How does a workout program apply to the world of private contracting, other than both companies keeping their people in shape?

MUSE

Agamemnon liked the business model—its methodology and belief in a competitive free market.

HOMER

What's the company's methodology?

MUSE

This is all open-source information listed on the company's website, but the genius is in the model's simplicity, and simple doesn't mean *easy*. It just means the model is not *complex*. All this program requires to open a gym in the company name is to attend a seminar and pay an affiliate fee. Then you can run your business any way that you see fit. Agamemnon was exposed to this functional fitness program during his time in the military, and he adapted their model to private contracting. And his idea was as genius and simple as Priam's—pay an affiliate fee, and you can come under the Hoplite umbrella. You can even run your contracting firm any way you want.

HOMER

What's the catch? There's always a catch.

MUSE

You're right. Here was the catch. In addition to the yearly affiliate fee, if your company accepted a contract, a percentage of those earnings were kicked back to headquarters upon completion of the contract. Conversely, if Agamemnon accepted a contract, he could subcontract it out to an affiliate. He'd charge a finder's fee to the subcontractor and take his cut off of the earnings of the completed contract.

HOMER

So, he basically created a continuous money stream between the affiliation fees and subcontract kickbacks?

MUSE

Correct. But that's not all.

HOMER

Of course. Please continue.

MUSE

Agamemnon also established a clause within the affiliation agreements, a similar clause seen in countries with military mutual defense alliances. If one contractor needed assistance, then all signatories were obligated to respond. Agamemnon essentially became a broker, and if he needed something done, he would just invoke the guaranteed assistance clause rather than use his own people.

HOMER

So, he doesn't work contracts anymore?

MUSE

No. He does. But only the most lucrative ones, or the ones with the lowest associated risk. It's like this—say he won a bid or accepted a contract for transportation of material or personnel through a non-permissive environment. Why would he use his own people and equipment when he could invoke that guaranteed assistance clause to use an affiliate company, a company that specializes in that type of work?

HOMER

It's a little cold-blooded, but I understand what he was driving at.

MUSE

And continuing with this hypothetical, Agamemnon technically took the contract—he didn't subcontract—so he would still get the lion's share of the profits and financially and operationally come out on top.

HOMER

Did this happen often?

MUSE

No, but it happened enough. The other affiliates got the message.

HOMER

And what message is that?

MUSE

That being with the best comes at a price.

HOMER

Why affiliate then?

MUSE

Because the affiliated companies make a higher profit than if they were operating independently.

HOMER

It still doesn't seem like a great deal to me.

MUSE

Sure, the first bite of your meal tastes like shit, but if you can choke it down, the rest tastes like filet mignon.

HOMER

You didn't affiliate. Why?

MUSE

Because I'm one of the few independents out there who can make it as a stand-alone entity.

HOMER

How?

MUSE

My private intelligence company specializes in ISR.

HOMER

For the record, what does ISR stand for?

MUSE

Intelligence. Surveillance. Reconnaissance. Like I said at the beginning of our interview, Fate does it all—from boots on the ground to eyes in the skies. For another company to do exactly what I do would be cost-prohibitive. Simple as that. Why affiliate when Hoplite just hires me directly? The same goes for Trojan or any other companies out there.

HOMER

So cost is the main reason the others affiliate?

MUSE

That, and affiliation provides brand recognition for the contractor and the customer.

HOMER

Brand recognition?

MUSE

A potential client who can't afford to hire Agamemnon, Menalaus, or Nestor directly may be able to afford a Hoplite affiliate.

HOMER

And what does that get them?

MUSE

A similar level of service at a more reasonable price point. Clients expect a certain level of quality and professionalism when they hire contractors. Just like with that functional fitness company from before, customers like to know what they're getting when they hire or acquire a brand name item, service, or product. At the end of the day, even though the affiliates run somewhat independently, Hoplite is a brand they trust. Priam proved his concept, and Agamemnon proved his. The free market would ultimately decide which one came out on top.

HOMER

Unless an event came along—organically or engineered—that would push one of those brands to the top and ruin the other.

MUSE

Exactly. And looking back on the events that followed, that's pretty much what happened when Zeus put out an open contract on Helen Argos.

ATTACHMENT 2

CASE NOTES: WORDS AND PHRASES DEFINED

AFFILIATION

- The state or relation of being closely associated with a particular person, group, party, or company.

MUTUAL AID

- An organizational model where voluntary, collaborative exchanges of resources and services occur to benefit the common good and/or a common cause.

MUTUAL DEFENSE PACT

- An agreement made between parties, most commonly nations, to support one another in the event of an attack.

- The goal of a mutual defense pact, alliance, or agreement is to ensure collective protection against an external threat.

SECTION 10

MUSE

When Zeus put out the open contract on Helen Argos, he probably thought he was hedging his bets. There's that old saying, "Two is one, and one is none," right? But what Zeus couldn't have foreseen—and what none of us could have foreseen—was that this thing would ultimately become the largest small-intensity conflict between private contractors the world had ever seen. Helen became a means to an end. She became a justification to fulfill personal agendas.

HOMER

But the situation didn't start out that way, did it?

MUSE

No, it didn't.

HOMER

How did it start?

MUSE

You know what really kicked this whole thing off? Two younger brothers, each trying to get out from beneath the shadows cast by their older brothers.

HOMER

You're referring to Paris and Menalaus, right?

MUSE

Yes, I am.

HOMER

Tell me about them.

MUSE

I'll start with Menalaus.

HOMER

That's fine by me. We just need to cover all the bases.

MUSE

Menalaus is a soldier through and through. All these guys are.
Before branching out to specialized elements, Agamemnon,
Menalaus, Priam, and Nestor all served together in conventional
units and in the special operations community. Menalaus lives
and breathes the warrior's creed. When everyone left the military and started contracting—first with Aegis and then with
Hoplite—he created his affiliate element and named it Spartan.

HOMER

Can you briefly describe Spartan as an entity?

MUSE

Spartan was a small-scale recreation of the main regiment
Menalaus operated with during his time in service.

HOMER

Can you be more specific?

MUSE

Imagine a top-tier, metropolitan police department's special
weapons and tactics team had a baby with a special operations
light infantry regiment, and that baby grew up to become one of
the best tactical units in the world—that was Spartan.

HOMER

What was Spartan's core competencies and mission-essential tasks?

MUSE

Spartan specialized in raids, extractions, renditions, and hostage rescues.

HOMER

I've also heard that Spartan participated in some shady, off-books stuff. What can you tell me about that?

MUSE

Unconfirmed reports say Spartan was contracted by both civilian and federal law enforcement agencies on multiple occasions to serve extremely high-risk warrants.

HOMER

I've heard those rumors as well. Do you think they're true?

MUSE

I don't know, and I don't really care. Menalaus was arguably one of the finest small-unit tacticians in the world, but off the battlefield, he has a reputation of not being the sharpest knife in the drawer.

HOMER

I've heard that about him, too.

MUSE

He's not dumb. He's just very socially awkward. His work in and out of the military would have been impossible if he weren't intelligent. Granted, he is the stereotypical pipe hitter, but he's also more than that.

HOMER

How so? Because from everything I've read and heard about him, I'm not seeing what you're seeing.

MUSE

To work with him is to know him. His tactical and operational IQ is through the roof. He just can't relate to so-called "normal people." He's like a professional athlete that way. You know how some guys and gals can go on to be broadcasters or analysts after their playing days are done?

HOMER

Yeah, I do. But some of those same folks can barely string together a sentence or verbalize a cohesive thought at a post-game presser.

MUSE

Right, but even those less verbal folks can deliver a master's class in the film room and on the field. That's Menalaus.

HOMER

But his brother is different, right?

MUSE

Yes. Agamemnon is like that rare athlete who can go on to become a coach or an on-air personality. And he always knew this about himself. Menalaus, on the other hand, didn't know his own limitations.

HOMER

Are you trying to say that he's not very self-aware?

MUSE

It's not exactly that. Menalaus, even though he was self-aware, had a chip on his shoulder. He wanted to show everyone that he was as smart and capable as his brother, that he could do everything Agamemnon could do but better. He was always in Agamemnon's shadow and could never seem to get out from under it . . . until the Helen situation came along.

SECTION 11

HOMER

Can you explain further what you mean by the Helen situation?

MUSE

Okay. On his own, Menalaus could never have pulled the job off. He needed an ally. A kindred spirit. So, who could he go to? He obviously couldn't go to his brother, and he couldn't go to Nestor. And before you ask, it's because Nestor is a diplomat and a peacemaker. He would've talked Menalaus out of any rudimentary plans.

HOMER

He needed to go outside of Hoplite. And he couldn't go to one of the affiliate companies because they'd snitch on him to Agamemnon. So, he came to you?

MUSE

Eventually. But remember, I only provide ISR resources and support. Nothing kinetic. And he needed kinetic.

HOMER

So, who did he go to? Who outside of Hoplite had the operational and tactical proficiency to adequately assist him?

MUSE

Paris.

HOMER

Menalaus went to Trojan for assistance? I find that hard to believe based on everything you've told me.

MUSE

No. Not Trojan. Not directly. Menalaus went directly to Paris.

HOMER

How did the two of them even meet?

MUSE

They met working on a contract together.

HOMER

What? How does that work?

MUSE

Spartan was hired to train a friendly host nation's elite-level special operations group in their particular mission-essential tasks. Archer, Paris' team, was hired to train the sniper element of that same special operations group in providing overwatch, on-site intelligence-gathering, and threat mitigation.

HOMER

And how do you know about this job?

MUSE

The same host nation that hired Spartan and Archer also hired my company to train its special operations drone operators. The nation's overall goal was to integrate this capability with the assaulters and snipers in combined force missions.

HOMER

You weren't kidding. You really are everywhere.

MUSE

Past. Present. Future. Don't let your fate be in someone else's hands.

HOMER

Catchy. You should put that on a business card.

MUSE

Already done—it's the company motto.

HOMER

Clever.

MUSE

Thank you. I came up with it all by myself.

HOMER

Anyway, back to the thing between Menalaus and Paris. How did their relationship develop? Wasn't the contract for Helen Argos already in place? Why would they even talk to one another? Didn't they hate each other?

MUSE

I'll work my way backward. Did they hate each other? No, not at that time. Remember, Agamemnon and Priam had a falling out, not these two. Menalaus backed his brother because that's what brothers do. There really wasn't any bad blood between the individual contractors of Hoplite and the employees of Trojan. Their relationship was more a friendly rivalry than anything else, like what you might see between cops and firefighters. Hoplite and Trojan frequently worked two parts of the same contract, and this host nation's training contract was one of those times.

HOMER

But why did they talk to each other? I still don't understand.

MUSE

Why did they talk to each other? They talked because it's what you do after the training day is over. Everyone gets together to eat, drink, and swap stories. As to your other question, wasn't the contract for Helen already in place? Yes and no, and this is where things started to go off the rails.

HOMER

Go on.

MUSE

When Zeus decided to go after Helen, he summoned Agamemnon and Priam to Olympus to discuss terms. At that meeting, Agamemnon was accompanied by Nestor. Priam was accompanied by Hector and Paris.

HOMER

Where was Menalaus?

MUSE

Purposely not included.

HOMER

Do you know why?

MUSE

If I had to guess, Agamemnon didn't want to bring his brother, who isn't too well-spoken, to a formal negotiation at the highest possible level.

HOMER

So where was Menalaus?

MUSE

Agamemnon sent him on some bullshit job to convenient-
ly get him out of the way. If Menalaus was busy, he couldn't be
an embarrassment.

HOMER

Again, how do you know that this meeting took place and
with whom?

MUSE

Because I was there, too.

HOMER

In what capacity were you there?

MUSE

To provide ISR in support of the Helen Argos contract.

HOMER

Doesn't Zeus have access to his own ISR platforms? Why did he
need yours?

MUSE

Really? How do you think things would play out in the media if
Zeus was exposed for using government manpower and equipment—all funded by the taxpayer—to track down a citizen and
former government employee? And moreover, how do you think
things would go if the public discovered that Zeus' whole motive
in doing so was to rendition this former employee to the blackest
of black sites and bleed her dry of the information and intelligence

she possessed . . . just to hide one of Zeus' many indiscretions?

HOMER

Well, when you put it like that . . .

MUSE

Does it still seem like a good idea to use government intelligence, surveillance, and reconnaissance platforms when he could just hire me?

HOMER

I hadn't thought in those terms before now. So, what was the pitch of the meeting?

MUSE

Remember when we started this debrief and I gave you my theory that Helen Argos was Zeus' daughter?

HOMER

Yes.

MUSE

Well, at that point, this theory was still alleged. The events that would unfold would eventually prove my theory correct, but at this meeting, the story was pitched to us as something completely different.

HOMER

And what was that story?

MUSE

Zeus presented us with evidence—which, as you know, was later found to be fabricated evidence—that a rogue intelligence operative possessed sensitive information and had threatened to sell that information to the highest bidder.

HOMER

What specifically were you told about this information?

MUSE

We were told that this information was so vital that if it fell into the wrong hands, the implications on national security would be catastrophic.

HOMER

Sounds very dramatic.

MUSE

A thriller writer couldn't have written a better story. Nothing like a good, old-fashioned threat that poses a clear and present danger to our way of life to stoke the flames of patriotism, and we fell for it. Hook, line, and sinker. After all, why would Zeus lie to us about something like this?

HOMER

So, Zeus laid out the story of a rogue intelligence agent who threatened to sell state secrets. What happened next?

MUSE

Zeus called Hermes into the meeting.

HOMER

Hold on. Are you saying the national intelligence director attended a clandestine, off-the-books meeting at Olympus? The same nighttime meeting that included Zeus and the heads of the three largest private military and intelligence contractors in the world?

MUSE

That's what I'm telling you.

HOMER

Wow, unbelievable. I guess you really can't make this stuff up. But back to the question: what was discussed?

MUSE

Solutions to the Helen Argos problem.

HOMER

What ideas were thrown around?

MUSE

Agamemnon, who's typically not averse to taking people's money and would gladly take Zeus', started with a very logical question.

HOMER

Which was?

MUSE

Why doesn't Zeus just throw a lightning bolt at her?

HOMER

Lightning bolt?

MUSE

That's code for armed unmanned aerial platforms dropping ordinance on people designated as enemies of the state. Warheads on foreheads. That type of thing.

HOMER

What was Zeus' response?

MUSE

Hermes fielded that question and explained to us that the rogue intelligence operative was not only a citizen but a former employee of one of his intelligence organizations, so a kinetic approach of this type was off the table.

HOMER

Seeding the lie with a little bit of the truth. Smart. What other options were considered?

MUSE

An improvised explosive device, a car bomb planted in her vehicle, a sniper, a staged robbery gone wrong, an accident made to look like a fall from a window or down a flight of stairs or an open elevator shaft, a staged drug overdose or suicide. The usual black bag stuff.

HOMER

Not that I'm condoning any of those . . . proposed methods . . . but these options seem like they would have been better than what ultimately transpired.

MUSE

True, but the real reason Zeus didn't have Helen assassinated, or have her "commit suicide," was his fear that Helen had some sort of dead hand in place.

HOMER

What's a dead hand?

MUSE

During a cold war period in our nation's history, our biggest and most dangerous adversary had a program called Dead Hand. The program allowed the automatic launch of nuclear weapons if certain conditions came to pass—one such condition being if that government's entire leadership team were killed. Zeus was afraid that if Helen was killed outright, then all of the information she possessed would somehow be released. No one knew at the time exactly what information she actually had, only that the leaking of this information could be disastrous for national security. This condition led Zeus to use contractors to capture and extraordinarily rendition Helen to a black site. This move would absolve Zeus and his administration of any official involvement and provide him with plausible deniability.

HOMER

So, I understand that you'd be hired directly to provide your services, but I still don't understand the competing contract aspect between Hoplite and Trojan.

MUSE

Simple. Zeus offered a prize.

HOMER

What?

MUSE

Zeus offered a prize to the first company to successfully complete the contract. That company would be guaranteed the right of first refusal on all future contracts originating from Olympus.

HOMER

Even with this huge threat looming over his head, Zeus was treating this whole thing like a game?

MUSE

Everything's a game to him. He thought he was running a game on Helen, but she ran a game on him. And now, he didn't want to get his hands dirty because of the potential political fallout or blackmail, so he pitted the two biggest and best contracting companies in the world against one another. He knew full well about the animosity between Agamemnon and Priam, and he used that animosity to his personal advantage—a win-win for Zeus. It didn't matter to him which company completed the contract, only that it was completed. Once Helen was captured . . .

HOMER

. . . Zeus would win. It's narcissistically brilliant. Not only would he win with Helen off the board, but he would win a private goon squad from the reigning company to clean up any future messes. You didn't want any part of that action? I find that hard to believe.

MUSE

Me? No way, man. That juice wasn't worth the squeeze. Besides, I was going to get a piece of that pie regardless, and I didn't have to subjugate myself to Zeus to get it.

HOMER

And how's that?

MUSE

The services Fate provides are too hard to come by and too cost-prohibitive to do on your own.

HOMER

Because you do ISR only, right? Nothing kinetic?

MUSE

Exactly. Observe and report.

HOMER

Now, please correct me if I'm wrong, but from my understanding in reading the after-action reports and debriefing transcripts from other subject interviews, wasn't the initial plan just to capture Helen?

MUSE

That's correct.

HOMER

And once captured, wasn't the plan that she would be turned over to Charon, who would bring Helen to Black Site Tartarus, where she would be questioned and interrogated by Hades?

MUSE

Correct again. But the term "plan" is a bit of a misnomer.

HOMER

Okay, then what would be a more appropriate term?

MUSE

Let's call it the *rules of the game*. Everything you've said so far has been right. The gist of the operation was to capture Helen alive, to turn her over to Charon, for Charon to ferry her to Tartarus, and for Hades to extract the national security information from her. *How* this operation was supposed to happen was left up to the individual contractor companies.

HOMER

Did Zeus have a plan to deal with the remainder of Helen's

network and her legitimate business holdings?

MUSE

He figured that once she disappeared, her network would collapse in on itself. The government would then weaponize the legal system to seize the remainder of her property and dismantle her businesses.

HOMER

What about her Dead Hand protocol?

MUSE

Nobody could definitively prove that she had one. Zeus and Hermes' concern was founded, but the more you think about it, the less it makes sense. Besides, even if she had a protocol of some kind, she probably had a live hand protocol.

HOMER

Can you explain the difference between live hand and dead hand?

MUSE

A dead hand is similar to a live hand, but the latter would require that Helen, or her designee, personally release the information into the wild.

HOMER

Can you elaborate?

MUSE

Sure. The situation was similar to what you see in the movies—someone has information, and he or she uses the information as leverage. The caveat is always that if that same person isn't heard from in twenty-four hours, then the information goes public. That type of scenario. But if Helen operated this way, she could never go away or do anything because she would always have to be there to reset her own personal doomsday clock, right?

HOMER

Valid point.

MUSE

A final reason a live hand was more likely than a dead hand: her type of information was priceless, but it could only be released once. If her information ever leaked unintentionally, Helen would gain nothing because she could no longer sell her compromising information as a complete package or in pieces.

HOMER

 So essentially, grabbing her was a calculated risk?

MUSE

Yes, a highly calculated one with all options weighed and considered, but ultimately a risk worth taking.

HOMER

So, the game was created. The rules were set and agreed upon, and I assume that in addition to the contractual language, non-disclosure agreements were drawn up and presented to the principles to be signed?

MUSE

Correct. But even that didn't go so smoothly.

HOMER

Of course it didn't. What happened?

SECTION 12

MUSE

Everything went pretty much like you just laid it out. Contract information, non-disclosure agreements, and all of this paper-work was slid in front of Agamemnon and Nestor. They signed without hesitation. But Priam called for a caucus with his sons.

HOMER

A caucus is not uncommon.

MUSE

No, you're right. It's very common in contract meetings, but in this instance, something felt off. The vibe in the room changed. I can't explain it, but it just didn't feel right.

HOMER

What happened next?

MUSE

I can only tell you what I saw and what I heard after. I wasn't in their conversation.

HOMER

Fair enough. Just lay the situation out for me from your point of view.

MUSE

Priam and his sons went into a secure huddle room to meet. They were in there for a while; and when they returned, Priam looked very calm, like he was completely at peace with a decision he had just made. Hector looked concerned but resigned. And Paris looked pissed.

HOMER

Why?

MUSE

Well, they came back and sat down at the table with Zeus, Hermes, Agamemnon, and Nestor. Priam signed the non-disclosure agreement acknowledging that nothing would ever be divulged about the operation to rendition Helen to Tartarus.

HOMER

But?

MUSE

But Priam pushed the contract back across the table and told Zeus and Hermes that Trojan would not be involved in any way, shape, or form. He thanked everyone for their time, got up, shook hands all around, and walked right out the door with his sons in tow.

HOMER

Holy shit.

MUSE

Holy shit is right. The silence in that room after Priam left was deafening. Priam's exit had sucked the air from the room and created a weird vacuum. The only question was who—or what—would fill it.

HOMER

Wasn't this a colossally bad move for Trojan? Priam might as well have just told Zeus go to fuck himself right to his face.

MUSE

Yes and no. Even if Trojan lost all their domestic contracts, the company had more than enough international business to operate for the long run. But you're right. The short-term fallout would be a tough storm to weather.

HOMER

What happened next? Obviously, Zeus' game changed. There used to be two teams—Hoplite and Trojan. Now there was only Hoplite. How do you play a game with only one team?

MUSE

Agamemnon hit Zeus and Hermes with a technicality. Hoplite, he said, wasn't one company like Trojan. Hoplite was made up of independently owned and operated affiliates.

HOMER

Where was Agamemnon going with this?

MUSE

He proposed that, as the head of Hoplite, he would sign the contract and the non-disclosure agreement, and then he would put the contract out to all of his affiliates. Whatever affiliate could capture and rendition Helen would win. Technically, he was right. This format still provided an open and competitive contract.

HOMER

Sounds like a rigged game to me. No matter what, Agamemnon would come out on top. What were the responses from Zeus and Hermes?

MUSE

Zeus was pissed. He looked at Hermes like this affiliate bullshit was something that should've been brought to his attention earlier. The last thing he wanted to do was put this sensitive information into even more hands. Hermes just looked like he wanted this whole mess to go away. A former employee trying to blackmail Zeus was not a good look for the nation's intelligence director.

HOMER

Planning a snatch-and-grab operation against a citizen under the guise of national security interests isn't a good look for the head of a nation either.

MUSE

Hey man, I'm not disagreeing with you. I'm just telling you what happened. The bottom line is that Agamemnon had them over a barrel. He knew it. They knew it. No one gave a shit about his affiliates before because Agamemnon's jobs were always magically completed. Out of sight. Out of mind. That type of thing.

HOMER

Kinda like how no one wants to know how sausage is made, right?

MUSE

Exactly. So, with no real choice, Zeus and Hermes reluctantly agreed. If they refused, then Agamemnon would possess information that he could use as leverage against each of them. They had no choice but to agree in order to avoid compounding an already bad situation.

HOMER

So how did the meeting end?

MUSE

It ended with Agamemnon getting what he wanted all along. Hoplite was awarded the contract to capture and rendition Helen to Tartarus.

HOMER

And like you said, no matter what happened, Agamemnon came out on top. No matter what affiliate got the job done, he won and even received the right of first refusal on all future contracts coming down from Olympus. Brilliant.

MUSE

But there were two variables that Agamemnon and Priam never foresaw or ever even seriously considered.

HOMER

And those were?

MUSE

Menalaus and Paris meeting up with one another.

SECTION 13

MUSE

Flash forward to where we were earlier. Menalaus, Paris, and I were working a foreign internal defense contract with that host nation's special operations group. We were sitting around the bonfire one night after a training day—everyone talking, bull-shitting each other, and having a few beers—when Helen Argos' name came up.

HOMER

How and why was she brought up?

MUSE

Well, Paris and Menalaus were both in their cups by that point. They started talking shop, bitching about never getting the good jobs, bitching about never getting the respect they felt that they deserved. Then, Paris brought up a big job that his dad and brother recently passed on. Menalaus then brought up a big job that his brother recently accepted. These casual mentions turned into one big mutual question.

HOMER

What was the job? I'm assuming that's the question, right?

MUSE

That's the one. Paris proceeded to tell Menalaus all about the Helen Argos job, and a plan began to form.

HOMER

What was the plan?

MUSE

The plan was that Paris and Menalaus would break away from Trojan and Hoplite and form their own private military contracting firm. Their first job together would be to take down Helen.

HOMER

That idea was pretty ambitious. But two things. First, wouldn't this plan violate the non-disclosure agreement? And second, if the operation was to be successful, then this newly formed contracting firm would be set. Neither Paris nor Menalaus would be dependent on Trojan or Hoplite anymore, correct?

MUSE

Yeah. The non-disclosure was technically violated. And this violation will play a larger role down the line. As for your second question, this plan, at its core, was basically a *fuck you* from Paris and Menalaus to the people they felt held them down and kept them back.

HOMER

And you partook in this new endeavor as well, right?

MUSE

You can't escape Fate. It's everywhere and everything, and for everyone.

HOMER

So, I've been told. But you did become part of this cabal, didn't you?

MUSE

Cabal's a strong word. They needed an ISR capability, and I was able to provide the service. And besides, I wasn't bound by any contract, non-compete, or non-disclosure clause. I'm a free agent. I will work with, and for, just about anyone. And if I'm hired, my number one and number two rules are made perfectly clear up-front.

HOMER

Confidentiality and no direct participation in kinetic operations.

MUSE

Correct. Complete compartmentalized confidentiality between involved parties. I provide the ISR. What is done with that information is the sole business of my client. I will not interfere, and I will not personally engage in kinetics.

HOMER

Some would argue that the only person who benefited from this entire debacle was you.

MUSE

Have I? Look around. I'm being debriefed at the highest possible level to give my full account of the biggest, most monumental clusterfuck of all time. And I'm the big winner?

HOMER

You can be. If you fully cooperate. And if you fully cooperate, you'll still be allowed to operate. That's the deal we've made with you. We'll uphold our end as long you uphold yours.

MUSE

I'm trusting you on that.

HOMER

Look, you're all about providing information. And according to you, what's done with that information is a matter of choice. Of free will. I have been authorized to provide you the same: a choice.

MUSE

There's that word again.

HOMER

We already have information on the clusterfuck, as you so colorfully named it, but we're looking for more information to fill in the blanks. That's where you come in. You are the only entity present on both sides, from beginning, to middle, to end. So yeah, in a way, I think you will be the one who does come out on top. You have a choice. You can be the last man standing. You could even call that fate.

MUSE

Well played, sir. Well played.

HOMER

I can be clever, too. But can we please continue?

MUSE

Yeah. I worked for most of the factions involved, and I know a good number of things. And yes, I will fully cooperate because not doing so is suicidal, both professionally and maybe even personally. But what we're about to discuss no one could have seen coming. What transpired would have been believed to be impossible.

HOMER

Good. As long as we understand each other. And don't make me remind you again about our deal, or it's off. Understand?

MUSE

I do.

HOMER

Good. Now, let's pick up where we left off. Tell me about Menalaus' and Paris' new venture and their plan to snatch Helen Argos out from under the nose of Hoplite. How could they do something like this without alerting Trojan that Paris had brazenly violated the non-disclosure agreement?

MUSE

They couldn't just immediately split from their parent organizations. They needed the infrastructure, resources, logistics, and personnel that Hoplite and Trojan had at their disposal. They first needed to pull off the big job to make the big lie come true.

HOMER

The big lie? What's that?

MUSE

The big lie is the one thing that every regular person has in common with the career criminal, the con artist, and the master thief. The big lie is based on that mythical big score—that one goal, achievement, or prize that would set someone for life. Getting the big score means living the life—getting to do whatever he or she wants, forever. Going after Helen Argos was the one big score Paris and Menalaus needed to make the big lie come true. Get it?

HOMER

Yes. What you're saying makes sense.

MUSE

No, it doesn't. It's all bullshit.

HOMER

What? Why?

MUSE

The big score doesn't exist. Even if it did, anything gained from those types of victories is usually squandered and lost. Look at all those fucking morons who win major lottery prizes. Multimillionaires—hell, some even become billionaires—all eventually lose the money. Somehow, they all piss it away.

HOMER

Then why believe in it?

MUSE

The big lie is what we all tell ourselves to get through the day. I figured this out a long time ago. But you've got to go through it to learn it.

HOMER

But Menalaus and Paris still believed in the big lie, so they thought the capture of Helen would be the big score to make their dreams come true.

MUSE

Yes and yes.

HOMER

And you felt no obligation to tell them otherwise?

MUSE

Did I feel like I was under some moral obligation to clue them in? No. You can tell someone not to do something—like telling a kid not to touch a hot stove—but that kid doesn't believe you until he experiences the pain himself. Kids get burned, but they learn the truth. This situation was no different. Menalaus and Paris needed to figure out the truth of the big lie for themselves. The only thing I could do was provide information for them to make decisions. What they did with that information was entirely up to them.

HOMER

Are you subtly referring to Project Icarus?

MUSE

You picked up on that, huh? Icarus was told not to do something because if he did, then bad things would happen. But what did he do? He ignored everyone and did the one thing he was told not to do.

HOMER

He flew too close to the sun . . .

MUSE

In a manner of speaking, yes, he did. And what happened? He crashed and burned. I know you think I'm duplicitous because of the way I operate, but at the end of the day, all of the choices we make are by free will. I don't force clients to do anything. They choose to do what they do. And they will live with the conse- quences of their actions—right, wrong, or neutral. I'm not the bad guy here. I just happen to be around when both good and bad things happen. I don't get any credit for the good; I just get blamed for the bad.

HOMER

I never considered your work from that point of view.

MUSE

Most people don't. Now, to be fair, did I benefit financially from working for Zeus, Hoplite, and Trojan? Yes. Did I benefit financially from working for Paris and Menalaus? Initially, yes. But did I benefit in the long term from this situation? No. Did anyone?

HOMER

I guess not. You bring up some excellent points. But let's get back on track, okay? Tell me more about Menalaus and Paris' plan.

MUSE

Okay. But first we have to discuss each man—his makeup, his psychology. And then you'll see how each player fits into the overall situation and subsequent aftermath.

HOMER

Sounds good. A breakdown like this might really prove useful down the road—not only as a way to understand why people do what they do, but also as a means to understand how their underlying motivations and psychology may even predispose them to certain outcomes. This whole situation—from beginning, middle, and end—will be a major case study one day. Once it's declassified, of course.

MUSE

You may be right. Let's start with Menalaus.

SECTION 14

MUSE

Like I've already said, Menalaus is a man of arms, a professional warrior to his very core. Tactically brilliant, but awkward in social and business settings. He's not comfortable with people outside of his peer group of like-minded individuals.

HOMER

Okay, you've already established these qualities . . . but what's he like?

MUSE

He's an excellent soldier and a steady, reliable man. He's moderate in stature. Auburn haired. Handsome. Once you get to know him, and he trusts you, he's got a surprisingly pleasing personality off of the battlefield and training grounds.

HOMER

But no matter what he does, he's overshadowed by his older brother, right?

MUSE

Right. He and Paris shared this problem. They each have the drive to get out from the shadows cast by their siblings so they can stand on their own merits. Menalaus has a deep, deep sense of honor. But Paris . . . he's an entirely different story.

HOMER

How so?

MUSE

He was the youngest son of Priam and Hecuba and the younger brother of Hector. He was well-grown and sturdy. Good nose. Good eyes. Black pupils. Black hair. Incipient beard. Long faced with heavy eyebrows. He had a big mouth, but he was charming and eloquent. He was very agile and an incredible marksman, but he was also cowardly and hedonistic. At least that's how Malalas, one of my intelligence sources, described him.

HOMER

Are there any other source accounts or descriptions of Paris?

MUSE

Dares Phrygian, one of my other guys, described him as tall and brave. He claimed Paris was swift and eager to take command. You might find this description weird, but Dares says that his eyes were beautiful and that he was also a charmer.

HOMER

You said a few things there that I'd like to explore.

MUSE

Okay. Which things?

HOMER

First, he was hedonistic. Second, he was cowardly. Third, he was eager to take command. These qualities don't seem to mesh together.

MUSE

Well, let's start at the top. He was hedonistic. Paris was devoted to the pursuit of pleasure. Even though he was engaged in a profession of arms, it was just a J-O-B for him. A means to an end. He made tons of money contracting and traveled all over the globe for his work. Rumor has it that he had a sidepiece in every major city around the world. Don't get me wrong—I'm not judging. But when you're just working contracting gigs to satisfy your pussy addiction, you might create problems with unforeseen effects. With me so far?

HOMER

I am. What about him being a coward?

MUSE

I believe that this part was taken out of context. Paris was not a coward in the true sense of the word. He was cowardly in the sense that when he did fight, he preferred to do it from a distance—preferably behind cover—and preferably with a tricked-out, high-caliber, high-powered rifle or bow.

HOMER

A bow? As in a bow and arrow? A crossbow? What are we talking about here?

MUSE

All of the above. Primitive. Longbow. Shortbow. Recurve. Compound. Cross—he was obsessed with archery. There are stories of him sniping people on jobs with bows. That was his thing. He was a sniper. He was lethal at a distance. He was not a pistoleer or rifleman. He was not a blade guy or a pugilist. He was not a judoka or a grappler. Would he fight like that if he had to? Yes. Could he fight like that if he had to? Yes. But he didn't prefer to be up close and personal. So, I think that's where this cowardly image of him comes from. Often, the sniper or the designated marksman is revered when he's on your side and feared and loathed on opposing sides. At the end of the day, I think the animosity toward Paris primarily came from the door kickers and assaulters who regularly get into the fight and mix it up close-quarters combat style.

HOMER

So, in a way, Menalaus and Paris were opposites of one another, but they also complemented each other? Like two sides of the same coin?

MUSE

Exactly. Menalaus was the consummate professional, and Paris was the consummate party boy. They needed one another to get out from under the shadows of their families.

HOMER

But how did these men differ?

MUSE

The difference was that Menalaus acted for honorable reasons. This plan was a means to an end so he could form his own company and completely devote himself to the perfection of his craft: war. For Paris, their alliance was a means to an end so that he could make even more money and completely devote himself to the perfection of his craft: pleasure.

HOMER

I guess one can't exist without the other.

MUSE

True.

HOMER

So, what about Paris' last descriptor, "eager to take command"?

MUSE

Yes, Paris was over-eager to take command. But again, context is important.

HOMER

What do you mean?

MUSE

Look, he was a young, good-looking kid with money. He certainly paid his dues, but he really didn't come up hard. He was placed into situations and environments that allowed him to succeed. Don't get me wrong, he earned what he was given; but he had this warped sense of reality about the world and his place in it.

HOMER

Can you elaborate?

MUSE

Paris wouldn't have been able to do this job on his own. His father laid the groundwork and opened the right doors for him. His brother pushed and pulled him through those doors and carried him along through their journey together. Paris had an overinflated sense of self-importance. He was smart, but not that smart. He was good physically and tactically . . . but not that good.

HOMER

What's the bottom line?

MUSE

The bottom line is that in Paris' mind, he thought that he could do a better job running Trojan than either his father or his brother.

HOMER

And that's what you meant by over-eager to take command?

MUSE

Yes. He believed he was entitled to command. I don't think the kid saw the forest for the trees—a recipe for bad decisions.

HOMER

Like trying to take down Helen Argos by himself?

MUSE

Exactly like trying to take down Helen by himself.

HOMER

Let's specifically discuss their plan to accomplish this goal.

MUSE

Okay, what do you want to know?

HOMER

Was the plan flawed in any way, shape, or form?

MUSE

No. The plan was solid, and the operation was executed flawlessly. What changed everything was what happened after the operation.

ATTACHMENT 3

CASE NOTES: WORDS AND PHRASES DEFINED

RENDITION

- The practice of covertly sending a foreign or domestic criminal, terrorist, or suspect to a location with less rigorous regulations regarding the humane treatment of detainees.

EXTRAORDINARY RENDITION

- The seizure and transfer of a person suspected of involvement with a terrorist group to another location for imprisonment and interrogation without due process of law.

NOTE

- *Rendition* or *extraordinary rendition* is sometimes referred to as *state-sponsored kidnapping*. This practice is typically illegal under international law.

SECTION 15

HOMER

Let's start with the concept of the operation and then move on to the execution. Sound good?

MUSE

Sounds good. The concept was simple, like they laid out in the initial meeting. Capture Helen Argos alive. Once apprehended, she would be delivered to Charon, who would render her to Tartarus. Finally, she would be interrogated by Hades. Mission success would be when Helen was in Charon's custody.

HOMER

That plan seems pretty straightforward.

MUSE

It was. But simple doesn't mean easy. The big variable was how much security she would have with her and around her.

HOMER

You're talking about her personal security detail as well as the physical security at each location she frequented? What can you tell me about possible target locations?

MUSE

Regardless of target location or security, the takedown needed to be quick, clean, and quiet. No one wanted to start a massive gunfight in the streets. Ultimately, they decided against taking her at her business headquarters.

HOMER

Why?

MUSE

For one, her headquarters was on the top floor of a large building that she owned. Two, it was in a downtown section of a major metropolitan area. Three, too much physical security guarded the place. Cameras, security doors, et cetera. Clean access and egress here would've been difficult. Fourth, Helen had too much personal security present around her at that location.

HOMER

What type of security are we talking about?

MUSE

Uniformed security guards in the parking garage underneath the building, uniformed guards manning the main lobby, and roving patrols of uniformed guards covering the interior and exterior of the building. And then you had a plainclothes personal security detail that was constantly close to her.

HOMER

What can you tell me about her personal security?

MUSE

These guys weren't run-of-the-mill security guards like the uniformed folks. These personal security detail agents were highly trained and highly skilled. Confronting them would have resulted in a major gunfight with a large body count. The threat matrix was too high on this location, so, they crossed it off the list. Though Menalaus and Paris could have executed the operation there if they had enough time to plan, prepare, and rehearse.

HOMER

Why do you say that?

MUSE

Because we would've had constant and ongoing ISR to determine security deployments, patterns of movement, camera placement, angles, and blind spots. We would've had the ability to study structural and infrastructural blueprints and schematics. But time was ticking away, and we were on the clock.

HOMER

What about secondary target locations, like homes and apartments?

MUSE

For similar reasons, her residences were also ruled out because of too many unknowns. One of the insurmountable problems with going after her where she lived was that she owned too many properties. In addition to her primary residence, she had apartments, condos, villas, chalets, and yachts all over the globe.

HOMER

Let me guess. Too many unknowns?

MUSE

Correct. Alarms, cameras, and sensor types were unknown. Camera placement and angles were unknown. Same with the number of personal security detail agents with her at any given time—all unknown.

HOMER

Bottom line assessment?

MUSE

The juice was not worth the squeeze at the primary or secondary target locations.

HOMER

What about a tertiary location?

MUSE

Helen owned and operated a club called the Golden Apple. This location rose to the top as a plausible place to apprehend her.

HOMER

Wouldn't the same problems be present at the Golden Apple?

MUSE

Yes and no.

HOMER

What do you mean?

MUSE

How much do you know about the Golden Apple?

HOMER

Nothing. This is the first time I've ever heard the name.

MUSE

Okay, let me tell you about this place. Prepare to have your mind blown.

HOMER

I'm all ears.

ATTACHMENT 4

CASE NOTES: LOCAL PRESS MEDIA EXCERPT

RELEVANT TEXT

International supermodel Helen Argos is accustomed to dominating the catwalks and runways of famous fashion shows and fashion houses worldwide, but now she's embarking on a whole new way to strut her stuff.

Multiple sources have confirmed that Argos will break ground on an ultra-swanky, members-only nightclub called Golden Apple.

When reached for comment about her devilishly delicious debut into the nightclub scene, the supermodel responded, "Not all fruit is forbidden, and I'm excited to be opening my first club in this world-class city. If you think you have what it takes, you may wind up with an exclusive invitation to come and play with me and my friends!"
This reporter may not have what it takes to rub elbows with the rich and beautiful, but I am certainly willing to take a bite out of whatever this catwalk icon serves up next.

SECTION 16

MUSE

Golden Apple isn't your typical nightclub or social club. It's an ultra-exclusive, ultra-selective, and ultra-secretive establishment.

HOMER

How do you join?

MUSE

Membership is by invitation only. That invitation simply grants you an interview. Your performance at that interview determines whether or not you can become a member . . . provided you meet additional criteria to join.

HOMER

What's the criteria?

MUSE

You have to be wealthy— generationally or new money.

HOMER

That's it?

MUSE

You also have to be powerful and influential in your respective field.

HOMER

Anything else?

MUSE

And you have to be someone who not only is connected but can also make connections.

HOMER

Golden Apple doesn't sound that much different than any other exclusive club. What makes this one so special?

MUSE

Golden Apple is where the most elite of the elites gather. They go there to be amongst themselves—to network, to make deals, to build up corporations and people . . . and to tear people down, as well.

HOMER

Sounds like a regular good ol' boy club.

MUSE

In some ways, it is, and in other ways, it isn't. The club is private. It's personal. But the extracurriculars Helen offers through Golden Apple are what keep customers coming back for more.

HOMER

And what exactly are these extracurriculars?

MUSE

Sex, in whatever way, shape, and form you can think of and with whomever you can think of. The place operates on pure, unadulterated hedonism and debauchery between consenting adults. And there are only two rules at Golden Apple.

HOMER

What are they?

MUSE

No animals. No kids.

HOMER

I guess that makes two redeeming qualities for Helen Argos.

MUSE

They're probably her only redeeming qualities.

HOMER

I still don't get the appeal. You can get sex anywhere. What makes Golden Apple so special?

MUSE

The beauty contests.

HOMER

Beauty contests?

MUSE

Quite possibly one of the most brilliant of Helen's honey traps.

HOMER

How do these contests work?

MUSE

My understanding is that members bid money to become judges.

HOMER

Is there only one contest? Or are there multiple contests taking place at once?

MUSE

Helen varied the schedule. Some nights, Golden Apple holds only one contest. Other nights, additional contests are held in the various VIP and private rooms.

HOMER

So, only one judge per contest?

MUSE

I believe so.

HOMER

How many contestants per contest?

MUSE

Three. For some reason, the number is always three.

HOMER

 And what's the cost to become a judge?

MUSE

I honestly don't know, but if you have to ask, you probably can't afford it. And if you can't afford it, then you're probably in the wrong place.

HOMER

Where does the money from the winning bid go?

MUSE

Believe it or not, Helen donated the money to a charity of her choosing.

HOMER

Do you believe that?

MUSE

I believe that the charity of her choosing was probably one of her many offshore bank accounts.

HOMER

I'm inclined to agree with you. But what's the deal? How does this whole thing work?

MUSE

Again, my understanding is that the judge and the three contestants go into a private suite where each contestant performs for the judge.

HOMER

Performs?

MUSE

Yeah, like the talent portion of an actual pageant, except these contestants demonstrate their unique . . . shall we say *skill set* . . . on the judge.

HOMER

Then what?

MUSE

After the talent portion ends, the judge awards the winner a prize.

HOMER

Seriously? A prize? Like a trophy?

MUSE

Yeah, but the prize is a solid gold apple.

HOMER

Are you for real?

MUSE

I shit you not. The winner receives a real, true-to-size, solid gold apple.

HOMER

This contest sounds like straight-up prostitution. How did this stuff benefit Helen? I mean, outside of her collecting and pocketing the money for the beauty contest?

MUSE

Those private VIP suites aren't so private. They're wired to record audio and visuals of the contests. Helen then used those audio and video files to extort the judges. She got them coming and going. No pun intended.

HOMER

Have you ever been inside Golden Apple?

MUSE

Me? No. But Paris had.

HOMER

Paris? Really? In what capacity?

MUSE

At first, he went for professional reasons. When Golden Apple first opened, he had a contract to train the personal security agents. He knows the physical layout along with the tactics, techniques, and procedures of the on-site personnel.

HOMER

Interesting.

MUSE

It gets better. What started as professional became personal. The way Paris told the story, he was a prospective member but didn't make the final cut. I don't think he was ever a judge, but knowing him, I'm sure he still managed to have a good time while he was there.

HOMER

So, Paris and Helen knew each other?

MUSE

Yes.

HOMER

Has Zeus ever been to Golden Apple?

MUSE

Zeus may think with his dick most of the time, but even he isn't that stupid.

HOMER

So, because of Paris' knowledge of Golden Apple, this location was heavily considered for the apprehension portion of the job?

MUSE

Yes. Golden Apple was a more workable option than her business headquarters or any of her homes.

HOMER

But Golden Apple was ultimately ruled out. Why?

MUSE

Again, the decision hinged on risk versus reward assessment. Menalaus and Paris knew they could take Golden Apple without a problem. Whenever Helen was there, she only had a minimal security detail with her.

HOMER

Why was that?

MUSE

Because too much security makes the members uncomfortable. If the members feel uncomfortable—like they're being watched—they're less likely to drink or enjoy the party favors. They would also be less likely to explore and experiment with their proclivities and fantasies.

HOMER

What about the security details of the members themselves?

MUSE

No extra security is allowed in. Security details drop their principals off, are directed to a detached building specifically designed for them, and wait for the call to go. They collect their principals once the party is finished. With security contained in that building, hitting the Golden Apple would have been easy.

HOMER

Okay, walk me through the details. Outside personal security is housed in a detached building on the grounds. And there's only a minimal personal security detail on Helen. I'm assuming there's also a minimal on-site security staff for the club itself?

MUSE

Correct. And the Golden Apple security staff is largely kept out of sight and out of mind. They are strategically hidden in key locations around the club and are called in as sort of a quick reaction force if one of the members gets out of hand.

HOMER

And were you aware of where these hidey-holes for the internal security staff were located?

MUSE

Paris knew, so yes. We were aware of these locations and how to deal with them.

HOMER

Sounds like this location would have made for an easy takedown. Why didn't the operation happen here?

MUSE

You're right. Golden Apple was very low on the threat matrix, but our risk matrix said differently.

HOMER

In what way?

MUSE

For this operation to succeed, there couldn't be any collateral damage. It had to look like Helen either disappeared on her own or was cleanly snatched. When Zeus said to take her alive, he wasn't suggesting. He was ordering. Helen needed to be gone.

HOMER

So, if Menalaus and Paris just started dropping bodies, that would have been a problem, right?

MUSE

The last thing we needed was to get into a gunfight with Helen's personal security detail or the Golden Apple internal security staff. But an even worse case scenario would be that during this hypothetical gunfight, a club member, some VIP, would catch a stray round. We would have had an even bigger incident on our hands.

HOMER

You seem like you want to say more.

MUSE

I do. If this had been a weapons-free operation, believe me, Menalaus would have gone in hard with his Spartans and smoked every living soul in Golden Apple, including the club members' security details in that detached building. Paris and his Archers would have been on the perimeter and provided sniper overwatch to take care of any squirters who somehow managed to escape.

HOMER

The capture certainly would have been over quickly, but the fall-out would have been impossible for even Zeus to contain.

MUSE

Correct. Too much risk; not enough reward. So, that's why we passed and chose our last option to apprehend Helen.

HOMER

And what was that?

MUSE

Motor vehicle interdiction.

HOMER

Can you define motor vehicle interdiction?

MUSE

Basically, it's the interception or prevention of a prohibited commodity like drugs, weapons, or explosives from moving around. Or a motor vehicle interdiction can be used to prevent the movement of a wanted person.

HOMER

Law enforcement has similar tactics, like felony motor vehicle stops or high-risk motor vehicle stops. Are these essentially the same?

MUSE

Yes and no. It's a safer way to arrest or capture someone. Taking someone in a vehicle is less risky than trying to breach and enter a structure, board an underway vessel, or dynamically enter and search an unknown area where the wanted person has a distinct advantage.

HOMER

Tactically, that makes sense. You lower both the threat and risk assessments. Plus, you only have to work within the confines and dimensions of a vehicle, where the person's movements are limited.

MUSE

Exactly.

HOMER

How exactly would this plan go down?

MUSE

When Helen traveled, she didn't use a large motorcade. In fact, she typically only used one vehicle. Usually, that vehicle was an up-armored SUV, locally sourced and locally available in whatever part of the world she happened to be in. She didn't attract undue attention to herself by riding in an exotic vehicle. She hid in plain sight.

HOMER

Smart. How many personal security agents did she typically travel with?

MUSE

Three. A driver, an agent in the front passenger seat who acted as the truck commander, and an agent in the backseat who served as Helen's immediate close protection specialist—her bodyguard.

HOMER

What if she wasn't alone?

MUSE

If she was personally entertaining someone, then the number dropped to just the driver and the truck commander.

HOMER

Were there times when she utilized more than one vehicle?

MUSE

Yes. At times, she had utilized a lead vehicle, her vehicle, and a trail vehicle. The lead and trail vehicles were packed with personal security agents.

HOMER

Numbers?

MUSE

For both the lead vehicle and the trail vehicle, you're looking at a driver, a truck commander in the front passenger seat, two to three agents in the rear passenger compartments, and one to two more in the cargo compartments. Those last two are affectionately known as gun monkeys.

HOMER

What were these extra vehicles for?

MUSE

These vehicles would come to the aid of Helen's vehicle if attacked. They'd disgorge their shooters to lay down suppressive fire while Helen was evacuated to a functioning vehicle. But, whenever she was at Golden Apple, or was moving between her business headquarters and home, she typically only traveled with one vehicle to keep a low profile. She didn't want to intimidate or scare her clientele or club members.

HOMER

But you didn't bet on Helen only using one vehicle, right?

MUSE

Correct. During the recon phase, we always planned for more

than one vehicle. We didn't want any surprises out there, and if we could find a way to easily deal with three to four vehicles, then one vehicle wouldn't pose an insurmountable problem. Hope for the best, but plan for the worst.

HOMER

Walk me through the defined roles and responsibilities for this operation.

MUSE

Sure. My role was to use my ISR platforms, along with intelligence-gathering methods like UAVs (unmanned aerial vehicles), HUMINT, SIGINT, ELINT, and RUMINT. That's human intelligence, signal intelligence, electric intelligence, and rumor intelligence, which my team used to cover and track Helen's movements—her schedule, itinerary, and location for a one-hundred-and-sixty-eight-hour period to establish a pattern of life.

HOMER

Why one hundred and sixty-eight hours?

MUSE

Because those hours equal one week. We call it the rule of one-sixty-eight. Once we were able to determine that she would be in town and at Golden Apple, we turned our attention to the actual planning and preparation for the apprehension, which would be handled by Menalaus.

HOMER

What would Paris' role be?

MUSE

Paris' job was to provide rolling surveillance of Helen once she went mobile. His team would form a moving perimeter around her to keep her contained.

HOMER

What was your assignment?

MUSE

I would provide the eye in the sky. Overwatch with my UAVs. If Helen deviated from her known routes, I would notify Paris, and the rolling perimeter would adjust and reform accordingly. Paris' Archers would also serve a secondary function once the interdiction stop was made.

HOMER

And what exactly was that secondary function?

MUSE

They would become a stationary blocking force that would close down streets, alleys, and other possible ingress and egress routes. Essentially, Helen would be trapped.

HOMER

What would happen next?

MUSE

Once the interdiction stop was made and Helen was apprehended, Paris and his Archers would disperse, driving off in different directions to a pre-established rendezvous point. There, they would ditch and sanitize their vehicles and equipment and then link up with Menalaus and his Spartans. Then they would all convoy to the meeting point with Charon. Charon would then ferry Helen to Hades, who would be waiting for her at Tartarus.

HOMER

I understand that Paris and his Archers had rolling perimeter, surveillance, and containment duty, but what tasking did Menalaus and his Spartans have?

MUSE

They would perform the actual interdiction stop.

HOMER

How would this be done?

MUSE

Are you talking about the actual tactics involved?

HOMER

Yes and no. I'm assuming that Paris and his Archers were probably rolling around in plainclothes and non-descript vehicles so that they could blend in while conducting their mobile perimeter. But how could Menalaus and his team get Helen's personal security detail to stop their vehicle and willingly turn her over?

MUSE

I'm not sure I completely understand your question.

HOMER

According to you, the whole reason her office, her home, or Golden Apple weren't selected was to avoid an incident. But short of crashing into her, how could you pull her over without creating the incident you were hoping to avoid? What thought was given to limiting potential witnesses and collateral damage?

MUSE

Excellent point. You're smart to have picked up on that discrepancy.

HOMER

That's why they pay me the big bucks.

MUSE

Do you remember the rumor I mentioned earlier? That Menalaus and his Spartans had allegedly been contracted to serve some high-risk warrants for certain federal, state, county, and local law enforcement agencies?

HOMER

Yes.

MUSE

Well, those weren't rumors. Menalaus and his team still had an inventory of law enforcement special weapons and tactics-type vehicles, uniforms, and equipment—all complete with the badging, patches, and decals.

HOMER

So, they posed as cops and essentially conducted a high-risk motor vehicle stop in the same manner that a tactical team would do to serve a high-risk warrant?

MUSE

Correct.

HOMER

And this method would almost guarantee that Helen's personal security detail would stop, because in their minds, they weren't about to run from the cops or have a shoot-out in the middle of the street?

MUSE

Exactly. Outside of a near-peer-level world leader like Zeus, any private security detail will stop when pulled over by law enforcement.

HOMER

Why?

MUSE

Because the people on those details need their jobs, and they won't jeopardize their careers over their clients. And we banked on that self-interest coming through here. We knew that the vehicle, or vehicles, would pull over and allow us to conduct our operation and be off with Helen. All her details would believe Helen was legitimately being arrested.

HOMER

Give me a sense of how the apprehension was supposed to go down, and we'll work backward from there if I have any follow-up questions, okay?

ATTACHMENT 5

CASE NOTES: LAW ENFORCEMENT PRESS RELEASE

RELEVANT TEXT

FOR IMMEDIATE RELEASE

The Metropolitan Police Department is seeking assistance from the public regarding a rash of motor vehicle thefts from various locations around the city.

Investigators have taken over a dozen reports of vehicles that have been stolen over a relatively short time period.

The thefts are believed to have been between the overnight and early morning hours.

All stolen vehicles were reported as late-model vehicles with no standard, on-board navigation/GPS systems.

Anyone with information is urged to call the Detective Bureau Auto Theft Desk.

SECTION 17

MUSE

I would operate UAVs over Helen's business headquarters, her residence, and Golden Apple to determine her routine and movements between those locations.

HOMER

Okay. Go on.

MUSE

Once I had those routines and routes established, I would wait for HUMINT, or human intelligence, to confirm her physical presence at Golden Apple on a specific date and time.

HOMER

What would happen next?

MUSE

Once that information was known, I would set up surveillance and give a warning order to Paris and his Archers. On my order, they would prepare to deploy to pre-designated staging areas and would position themselves to start rolling perimeter surveillance of Helen as she left Golden Apple.

HOMER

Why not take her en route to Golden Apple?

MUSE

Her not showing up might raise suspicion, so we decided that taking her after she left would be better. We planned the apprehension for very late at night or very early in the morning. Less traffic. Plus, fewer pedestrians equal less risk.

HOMER

Makes sense. Please continue.

MUSE

Once Helen and her security detail left Golden Apple, I would continue to provide aerial overwatch via UAV, while the eyes-on, rolling surveillance and cordon would be turned over to Paris and his team.

HOMER

What would the function of each particular element be?

MUSE

My primary function at this point would be to provide the ground units with advanced warning of any legitimate law enforcement action in the area, as well as any traffic crashes, road work, road closures, or detours. I would also monitor for counter-surveillance or counter-abduction assets that Helen may have utilized.

HOMER

Okay. I understand your function, but please describe what Paris and his team were actually doing at the time this thing kicked off.

MUSE

Here's the best way I can explain the setup—picture Helen and the vehicle she was riding in as being in the middle of an open area. Does that make sense?

HOMER

Yes.

MUSE

Now, picture vehicles surreptitiously surrounding her, not close enough to be seen, but not so far away that they can't keep tabs on her. She's being constantly monitored through cross streets, intersections, and breaks between structures. Are you getting the picture?

HOMER

I am.

MUSE

Now, picture both elements—Helen and Paris—moving simultaneously through the operational area. In other words, Paris and his Archers were basically riding herd on Helen. They kept her in the middle as they moved along with her.

HOMER

How were the Archers set up?

MUSE

Like compass points, but points that moved and shifted as she moved and shifted. No matter where she went, a vehicle was north, south, east, and west of her position.

HOMER

Got it. What were you doing?

MUSE

I fed them real-time updates from my UAVs. Any relevant information was sent directly to BLUFOR and OPFOR tracking units in the surveillance vehicles so they could rotate accordingly.

HOMER

What are BLUFOR and OPFOR?

MUSE

Think of BLUFOR, or blue force, as the good guys and OPFOR, short for opposition force, as the bad guys. These tracking devices monitor who is where on the battlefield to avoid friendly fire or fratricide.

HOMER

Earlier, you mentioned the possibility of counter-surveillance, counter-ambush, and counter-abduction teams doing pretty much the same thing as Paris, but in reverse. What was the plan to deal with them?

MUSE

One of my roles was to call out and mark any of these units if they appeared.

HOMER

Okay. What about Paris? What would he do?

MUSE

Paris and his team had a redundant role on the ground level. They would also monitor for counter-surveillance, let me know if they found something, tag those units, and send their positions to the entire team.

HOMER

What would happen if one of these units was seen, marked, and tagged?

MUSE

We'd send our closest unit to deliberately crash into the counter-unit, a move that would be passed off as an ordinary car accident. Taking out one of their units would keep us in the game longer.

HOMER

Bold move. Sure, you take out one of theirs, but you also lose one of yours. And what if the targeted unit doesn't buy that what happened was just an accident?

MUSE

You're right, we'd be taking a risk, but a calculated one. Intelligence estimates had Helen's counter-units at two to three vehicles at the most, whereas we had eight vehicles rotating and revolving around her vehicle.

HOMER

So, this was basically a numbers game? Am I correct in saying that?

MUSE

Yeah, what you're saying isn't wrong. Realistically, Helen couldn't have eight counter-units doing what we were doing—too many vehicles trying to occupy the same space at the same time. It's not only against the laws of physics, but that many vehicles would have drawn attention.

HOMER

Go on.

MUSE

Now, if we had been operating in a high-risk environment, then these counter-units would've been almost a certainty. That, and she would have been moving in a much larger, up-armored motorcade. But we were on her home turf, in a low-risk, permissive environment. She was moving between known and familiar locations, through friendly routes.

HOMER

So, there wouldn't be anything out of the ordinary that would trigger a threat response from Helen's security detail? Interesting. Do you think her security team was too complacent?

MUSE

No. I think they were operating in the environment they found themselves in. Also, the operators on Paris' team were in plainclothes, driving nondescript, common vehicles. The personnel chosen for this task were literally the definition of the gray man or gray woman. They completely blended into their surroundings and looked like they belonged. The gig would have been up if we had used the stereotypical operator to conduct this plan—I'm talking large, muscular, bearded guys with wraparound shades, backward ball caps, worn jeans, and tight t-shirts.

HOMER

So, Paris' team was hiding in plain sight?

MUSE

Yes. That's why Paris and his Archers performed this task and not Menalaus and his team. It's another part of what made Paris really good at what he did. His bailiwick was sniping, counter-sniping, recon, and intelligence gathering in all kinds of environments across the world.

HOMER

I guess Menalaus wouldn't make sense for a job like this. He seems more like a sledgehammer, and Paris a scalpel.

MUSE

Paris and his team were ghosts. They got in and operated in plain sight. They got out when the job was done. And the most brilliant part is that Paris had a complete sub-unit of all female Archers— they call themselves the Amazons—and they were heavily utilized for this operation.

HOMER

I've never heard of the Amazons before. What can you tell me about them?

MUSE

Try picturing this. You're one of Helen's counter-units, and you crash into a car full of females who are all dressed to the nines, women who look like they're coming from, or going to, the clubs or the bars. Even if you radio in that you've been hit, how suspicious are you going to be when three or four attractive girls are crying and carrying on about their wrecked car?

HOMER

Good point.

MUSE

Would we be down a vehicle? Yeah, but it's one vehicle out of eight. Would they be down a vehicle? Yup, but for Helen's team, third or half of their counter-units are now off the table. It's simple math, and the numbers were on our side. The risk was worth the reward.

HOMER

Were any of these counter-units discovered?

MUSE

No. On the date and time of the operation, Helen was in a single vehicle—an SUV with three personal security detail agents. These agents included a driver, a front-seat passenger who was the team lead, and a close protection agent riding in the backseat passenger compartment with Helen.

HOMER

No gun monkeys in the cargo area?

MUSE

No gun monkeys. She was traveling light.

HOMER

Okay, so once Menalaus initiated the traffic stop, what was the role of Paris and his Archers?

MUSE

Once the stop was made, they'd lock down the outer perimeter and act as a blocking force. They were also provided with forged law enforcement credentials and those ubiquitous windbreakers with screen-printed lettering on the front. They were instructed to tell passersby that a law enforcement operation was underway and that access to the area was temporarily shut down.

HOMER

What if real cops happened by?

MUSE

Paris' team would bullshit 'em and dazzle 'em with their fake creds until they went away.

HOMER

And if the cops didn't leave?

MUSE

Most beat cops will believe what they're told by other people who can talk the talk and are displaying realistic-looking creds. They may hang around a bit, but once they find out they won't need to file or write any reports, they'll be on their way.

HOMER

How could you be certain?

MUSE

It's well-known that law enforcement agencies don't communicate with one another. Some secret squirrel task force is always running around doing secret squirrel shit, and the last people to find out are the patrol cops.

HOMER

But still, what if real cops happened to come up on the scene and got suspicious?

MUSE

Like I said before, Paris and his Archers could walk the walk and talk the talk. They knew how the game was played. And besides, they wouldn't start killing cops. Injure them? Sure. Incapacitate them? Yes. But kill them? No. No way.

HOMER

Okay. Makes sense. Now, the stop is made, the takedown is

complete, and Helen is in custody. What was Paris' and the Archers' next move?

MUSE

They would disperse. Head in different directions. Dump and sanitize the vehicles. Make their way back to the link-up point.

HOMER

What were you to do?

MUSE

Remain on station with my UAVs and provide overwatch for Menalaus and his team as they exfiltrated with Helen and made their way back to the rendezvous point.

HOMER

Where was the rendezvous point?

MUSE

The port. That's where we were to meet Charon and where he would take custody of Helen. Zeus would then be notified that the mission was a success. From there, Helen would be ferried to Tartarus.

HOMER

Wait! Is Tartarus a *boat*?

MUSE

Yes, Tartarus is a floating black site, and according to contractor lore, Tartarus sails across the River Styx to Hades and the Underworld. Even weirder, the rumors say that those who board Charon's ferry cease to be human and become shades. They never return.

HOMER

No one ever comes back?

MUSE

To my knowledge, no one's ever returned from Tartarus or the Underworld. While the information being extracted from a person might make it out, the actual person never leaves.

HOMER

Do you believe these rumors?

MUSE

I do now. Before this operation, I thought the whole Hades, Underworld, and Tartarus thing was exaggerated, you know? It's sort of like a campfire boogeyman tale that keeps getting more outlandish with each telling. No one I've ever worked with or for had actually ever seen Charon. And no one I knew had ever seen Hades. Sure, we'd heard those names and the stories. But this operation was the first time—for me, anyway—the truth came out. Before this contract, I thought these stories were shit-talking to keep people in line.

HOMER

Before we move on to Menalaus and the actual takedown, I want to spend time on Charon, Tartarus, Hades, and the Underworld. This information is all new to me. What can you tell me? And please, include rumors, legends, and your personal perspective.

MUSE

Charon is a psychopomp.

HOMER

A what?

MUSE

A psychopomp. A guide. He escorts people from our world, the real world, to the Underworld. Or, in this case, to Tartarus. He's what you would call a secure transportation specialist.

HOMER

What else can you tell me about him?

MUSE

He doesn't cast judgment on people. He just transports them from Point A to Point B. He's kind of weird, too.

HOMER

Weird? How?

MUSE

Think about it. He's got a pretty fucked up job. He takes people on a one-way trip to a place he knows they'll never leave. Not to mention, who knows exactly what happens to those people while they're in the Underworld? I'd be a little weird, too.

HOMER

Yeah, but what makes him weird?

MUSE

He's got this thing . . . it's strange . . .

HOMER

What type of thing?

MUSE

He charges two coins per passenger for his ferry rides.

HOMER

Coins?

MUSE

Doesn't matter the currency or the denomination, but the cost to cross over to the other side is two coins.

HOMER

Who pays him, and what's he do with the coins?

MUSE

I don't know, and I don't care. I wasn't about to ask him.

HOMER

Fair enough. What does he look like?

MUSE

Rough. Unkempt. Bearded. His eyes look hollow but burn with this intensity, like they're on fire. They're creepy as hell. He's creepy as hell.

HOMER

How would you describe his demeanor? His personality? Things like that?

MUSE

He's testy. He'll get rough with his passengers if they don't move fast enough. He doesn't like hanging around a place for too long. He's definitely a professional. He wants to come in, pick up his package, and be on his way. He's highly skilled, too. The guy can drive, pilot, or fly anything—doesn't matter what conveyance he uses. He will deliver his cargo to Hades on time—from anywhere in the world—plus or minus thirty seconds. That's his guarantee. For this operation, he happened to be piloting a skiff to take Helen to Tartarus.

HOMER

Can you describe what happened on the day of the operation?

MUSE

I was already at the rendezvous point with my team. Charon was there, too. My team and I had prepositioned ourselves there to secure the location and to run flight operations. We were all waiting for Menalaus to get there with Helen so the hand-off could be made. Out of all the operations I've ever been involved in, this experience was the most awkward and surreal. Here I am, trying to monitor and run our UAV overwatch. At the same time, I'm looking over and seeing Charon just sitting there. Not talking to anyone. Not really moving. Just sitting there. Raw dogging the whole thing. Staring straight ahead while taking small sips of black coffee. When someone asked him a question, he'd slowly turn his head, stare right through them, and then slowly nod his head one time for yes or twice for no. But I could tell he was getting pissed.

HOMER

How could you tell?

MUSE

You could just tell from his face. His expression would get darker and meaner the longer he was there.

HOMER

Why?

MUSE

Because you could feel that this operation was taking way longer than it should've. I knew it, and I sure as hell knew that he
did, too. A feeling hung in the air that things weren't going to
end well.

HOMER

We'll get to what happened, but I want to switch gears quickly.
Let's talk about Hades. What do you know about him?

MUSE

Not much. Only what I've heard. Like I said, I've never met him.
I don't know anyone who has. I've never worked for him, either—
just so we're clear.

HOMER

We're clear. But what have you heard?

MUSE

I've heard he's Zeus' brother. I've also heard that he doesn't come
around Olympus much.

HOMER

Why?

MUSE

My opinion?

HOMER

Yeah.

MUSE

I think it's because Hades—or the thought of him and what he does—makes people very uncomfortable.

HOMER

We don't know much about him, either. But that's definitely the vibe we're getting as well. We're trying to build a dossier on him. What have you heard about his personality and demeanor?

MUSE

I've heard that he's stern and shows no pity or empathy. He can't be bought or bribed. He can't be reasoned with. He's unmoved by prayers or begging. But oddly enough, all these qualities aren't necessarily negative if you stop to think about it.

HOMER

Why do you suppose that is?

MUSE

Honestly? I think Hades sees himself as the person who maintains the balance between good and evil. Just like Charon. Somebody has to do what he does. And apparently, no one else was lining up to run the Underworld . . . so why not him?

HOMER

Good point. But Hades' whole job does seem a little woo-woo to me.

MUSE

Yeah, it seemed that way to me, too. But then I found myself directly involved in an operation that he and Charon played a pretty big role in. Your opinion changes pretty damn quick when you're up close and personal with the mystical.

HOMER

What else can you tell me about Hades?

MUSE

I've also heard him described as passive, but not in a weak or submissive way. More like indifferent.

HOMER

Indifferent? How so?

MUSE

I'm just speculating here, but he seems to go about his role quietly. He's not the guy who decides who goes to the Underworld or Tartarus. He just accepts whoever gets sent to him.

HOMER

And once the passengers arrive?

MUSE

He judges them, firmly but fairly. At least that's how the story goes.

HOMER

Interesting—I hadn't considered Hades as really more than some evil, one-dimensional character.

MUSE

I also think that what the majority of people forget is that supplanting Cronos and his regime took Zeus and his brothers ten years, and now Helen threatened to throw all that work away.

HOMER

And Zeus will do everything he can to keep his power. Even send someone to Hades?

MUSE

There's no way Zeus is ever giving up Olympus. I'm sure he reached out to his brother and was like, "Hey, I have a problem, and I need your help. I'm sending you someone who has information that can bring me down. Extract that information from her any way you can and forward it to me." And I'm sure, Hades was like, "Sure thing, bro. Once you capture her, I'll have Charon bring her to Tartarus, and I'll get what you need from her."

HOMER

Which brings us back to the plan to apprehend Helen before I asked you about Hades.

MUSE

Exactly. My team and I, along with Charon, are all waiting at the rendezvous point safe house. We were waiting for Paris and his Archers, but also for Menalaus and his Spartans to arrive with Helen so that Charon could ferry her off to a fate I wouldn't wish on my worst enemy.

HOMER

Okay, but before we get there, let's talk about Menalaus' part in this operation.

ATTACHMENT 6

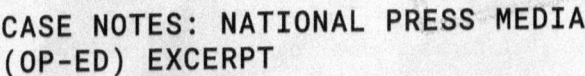

CASE NOTES: NATIONAL PRESS MEDIA (OP-ED) EXCERPT

RELEVANT TEXT

Fear goes by many names around the world—Baba Yaga, Baboulas, and the Boogeyman, to name a few. We've been told by our parents that monsters aren't real. But what if monsters are real, and these monsters aren't frightening humanoids but instead locations—actual, physical locations funded by your tax dollars? And like with the fear of monsters, these places exist all around us but somehow remain hidden.

Make no mistake, these places I'm talking about are just as scary as those things that go bump in the night. But unlike the nocturnal nemeses that our childhood minds conjure up, these places are real, and they have a name every bit as unnerving as the thought of Baboulas eating misbehaving children: black sites.

Black sites, as their politically correct definition states, are clandestine detention centers. But the correctness and niceties end there. These sites are operated by, or on behalf of, nations whose people have not been charged with any crime. These same people are locked away without due process or access to legal representation. Essentially, the Boogeyman steals people away in the dead of night.

Black sites are an open secret in the military and intelligence communities, and I suppose if you're not a terrorist or an enemy of the state, then you have nothing to fear. But what happens when your government unleashes these monsters on their innocent, everyday citizens? Citizens who may have run afoul of the powers that be? Citizens who now suddenly find themselves kidnapped—excuse me—"renditioned" to one of these sites by their own government, a government sworn to protect and defend their basic human rights? Would you worry then?

Tread lightly and speak carefully, Citizen. Check under your bed and in your closet before you go to sleep tonight. Be good. Behave. Ask no questions. Do that, and you may wake up in your room, not in some pitch-black cell, never to be seen again.

SECTION 18

MUSE

Everything was on schedule according to the timetable laid out for the plan. I had UAV overwatch up and running. Paris and his team had Helen contained within his moving perimeter. There weren't any counter-units in the area of operations. Helen was traveling in one SUV with three personal security detail agents—a driver, a front-seat passenger team lead, and a single close protection agent in the rear passenger compartment with her. In our planning phases, we had drawn this exact situation up as the best-case scenario.

HOMER

What can you tell me about the takedown?

MUSE

During our recon phase, we established a relatively isolated area that Helen had to drive through. This spot was designated as the takedown location. Menalaus and his Spartans were prepositioned to execute the stop once Helen's vehicle entered the kill zone.

HOMER

Kill zone?

MUSE

Sorry. Poor choice of words. Once Helen was on the X, Paris and his team locked down the outer perimeter while I maintained UAV overwatch and Menalaus initiated the interdiction stop.

HOMER

And Menalaus' team was outfitted with tactical law enforcement uniforms, equipment, and vehicles, correct?

MUSE

Yes. Three vehicles. Blacked-out SUVs complete with push bumpers, heavy-duty shocks, brakes, tires, recessed emergency lights, wigwags, strobes, takedowns—the whole nine yards.

HOMER

Got it. What happened next?

MUSE

Once the command to execute was given, Vehicle One would pull in behind Helen's SUV and activate its blue lights, just like any cop would if they were pulling someone over. And remember, Menalaus' vehicles were the same make and model used by virtually every law enforcement agency in the country, so there wouldn't be any reason for Helen or her driver to doubt that this traffic stop was anything beyond the routine.

HOMER

Okay. Vehicle One initiated the stop, and Helen's SUV pulled to the right and came to a complete stop, correct?

MUSE

Correct. Vehicle One was directly behind and slightly offset to the left of Helen's rear bumper. Vehicle One turned out its tires to catch any stray rounds in the unlikely case of a gunfight.

HOMER

How far back was Vehicle One from Helen's SUV?

MUSE

Thirty-five to forty feet, give or take.

HOMER

What action did Vehicle One take?

MUSE

The driver and front-seat passenger of Vehicle One both got out and moved to the rear corners of their vehicle. The operator on the passenger's side rear corner took up a long, lethal cover position on Helen's vehicle. That operator's sole job was to provide overwatch and address any threats that might have emerged from the target vehicle. The operator who was driving took up a position on the driver's side rear corner and acted as part of the arrest team, while also providing cover when not actively going hands-on with the occupants of the target vehicle.

HOMER

What about Vehicle Two?

MUSE

Vehicle Two pulled up alongside Vehicle One, maybe about ten or twelve feet away and to the left. Vehicle Two's nose was more or less pointed at the driver's side rear corner of the target vehicle's bumper. The operator in the front passenger seat of Vehicle Two took up a position at the rear passenger side corner and also acted as part of the arrest team. He would provide cover when not actively apprehending any occupants from the target vehicle. The driver of Vehicle Two would move to the rear corner on his side of the vehicle and provided additional long, lethal cover.

HOMER

Vehicle Three?

MUSE

Vehicle Three would pull alongside Vehicle Two's left and act as the command and control vehicle. The driver of Vehicle Three would have the best view of the target vehicle and would be the person who gave all of the commands to the occupants of Helen's vehicle. The additional operators in Vehicle Three provided cover and assisted personnel in apprehending the target vehicle occupants. They also provided scene security for the inner perimeter while the interdiction stop was conducted.

HOMER

So, all the vehicles were set. What happened next?

MUSE

Once all of the vehicles were set and all of the operators in place, visual and verbal confirmation was given and relayed to the takedown commander, who then began issuing commands to the occupants of Helen's vehicle. This process is highly choreographed and methodical and takes a little longer to pull off than a motor vehicle assault.

HOMER

Why not just assault the vehicle and be done with it?

MUSE

That idea was briefly discussed, but the risk of collateral damage and harm to Helen was too great. And besides, the tactics we employed are used worldwide, so nothing we did would attract any suspicion from her security detail.

HOMER

What do you mean?

MUSE

If her security detail thought they were under attack, they'd react accordingly. They'd defend her and counterattack against an assault. But here, using high-risk motor vehicle stop tactics, they'd think they were being legitimately stopped by law enforcement.

HOMER

You said that Menalaus was on-scene? Where was he positioned?

MUSE

Vehicle Three, but he wasn't the one who would be giving commands during the stop. He was acting in a command and control capacity. He had overall command, but he was observing and ensuring his people were in the best possible positions at the right time for maximum efficiency, operationally speaking.

HOMER

What happened next?

MUSE

Once everyone was set, the interdiction team commander gave very clear and precise instructions to the driver of Helen's vehicle.

HOMER

What type of instructions?

MUSE

Putting all the windows down, having everyone inside place their hands out of the windows or on the headliner, turning the engine off, taking the keys out of the ignition, and then placing the keys outside of the vehicle, either on the roof or the ground. Once those actions had been completed, the team commander would announce the fictious arrest warrant for Helen Argos, and then each person in the vehicle would be ordered out, one at a time, starting with the driver. From there, every other person would be ordered out of the driver's side of the vehicle and individually walked back in between Vehicles One and Two, where they'd be handcuffed, searched, and detained.

HOMER

What would have happened if someone got out on the passenger side?

MUSE

The long, lethal cover positioned at Vehicle One would view that as a hostile act—being made with hostile intent—and would address that threat aggressively. But before the order-outs and call-backs began, the team lead warned the occupants of this. So, they started stepping out of the car, one by one, as they were ordered.

HOMER

Who was last to be ordered out?

MUSE

Helen.

HOMER

So, once she was ordered out—called back, handcuffed, and searched—what happened?

MUSE

She was placed in the passenger side rear seat of Vehicle Two. Her security detail was cuffed and lay prone on the ground behind Vehicle Two, with the driver of Vehicle One covering them. In keeping up the ruse that this was an actual police action, Helen's vehicle was then cleared.

HOMER

What does that process entail?

MUSE

The team lead would give a ghost call out to whoever was left in the vehicle. The long, lethal cover would be left in place, and a two-man team would be sent at a perpendicular angle along the driver's side of the suspect vehicle. The team would clear Helen's SUV as they went from the back to the front.

HOMER

Why?

MUSE

Because this way, there would be no risk of crossfire. Together, the agents' positions created an L-shaped field of fire. Long, lethal cover could fire straight ahead at the rear of the suspect vehicle, and the clearing team could fire into the vehicle from the opposite side. This positioning also guaranteed no friendly fire.

HOMER

Was anyone found in the vehicle?

MUSE

No. It was clear.

HOMER

What happened next?

MUSE

The passenger area and front-seat areas were cleared. That only left the rear cargo compartment.

HOMER

And how was that cleared?

MUSE

The clearing team would signal to the long, lethal cover man that they were going to pop the hatch. Once the cover man was set, the hatch would be opened, and the cover man would have a clear sight line into that area. If fire was necessary, the clearing team and cover man would still be set up in an L-shaped field of fire.

HOMER

Was anyone back there?

MUSE

No. The compartment was clear. The whole vehicle was clear.

HOMER

Then what happened?

MUSE

Vehicle Two had Helen, and they drove away, followed by Vehicle One.

HOMER

What about Vehicle Three?

MUSE

Vehicle Three stayed on-scene to deal with Helen's personal security detail.

HOMER

How was that handled?

MUSE

I don't know.

HOMER

What do you mean, you don't know?

MUSE

By that time, I had released my UAV coverage from the take-down scene to follow Vehicles One and Two as they made their way back to the rendezvous point.

HOMER

Okay, so there was no aerial overwatch on Vehicle Three. Still, do you know what was briefed to her detail regarding the on-scene situation?

MUSE

As planned and rehearsed, the lead operator in Vehicle Three would explain to the security detail that there was a warrant for Helen Argos and that she was going to be taken to a detention facility where she would be booked, fingerprinted, and photographed. Her detail was also told that after the booking process, she would then be allowed to make her one phone call. Finally, the agents were informed they could take their SUV and leave, the lead operator made sure to thank them for their cooperation and patience. In other words, our guys followed the exact procedure for a real arrest.

HOMER

Okay, so Vehicles One and Two headed for the rendezvous point, right? Vehicle Three remained on-scene, thanked the security detail for their cooperation, and then kicked the detail loose, correct? Did Vehicle Three also make its way back to the rendezvous point?

MUSE

Yes, but by a different route.

HOMER

Did Vehicle Three successfully return to the safe house rendezvous point?

MUSE

Yes.

HOMER

Did Vehicles One and Two?

MUSE

No.

HOMER

What happened to them?

MUSE

Paris.

SECTION 19

HOMER

What do you mean?

MUSE

Thumbnail sketch?

HOMER

For now, but I'm going to have follow-up questions.

MUSE

I don't doubt it. Vehicle One became immobilized. Vehicle Two became isolated. He took out my UAV coverage. Vehicle Two was taken down. Paris made off with Helen Argos. Bottom line: he fucked us.

HOMER

Who do you mean by us?

MUSE

Me and Menalaus.

HOMER

Can you be more specific?

MUSE

For me, the fucking was purely financial. Paris used my capabilities and platforms to get Helen apprehended. When he double-crossed me, he just stiffed me on the fee. But he really used Menalaus and took advantage of him.

HOMER

How so?

MUSE

He didn't have the gear, equipment, or muscle that Menalaus had. Paris and his Archers couldn't do what Menalaus and his Spartans did. The reverse isn't necessarily true, though. Certain Spartan elements can perform the same mission set as the Archers. They're not as good, but they'll get the job done. If push came to shove, Menalaus could've pulled this job off. His way wouldn't have been pretty—maybe even a little messy—but he would've gotten the job done.

HOMER

But he didn't know about the job until Paris brought it to his attention, right?

MUSE

Correct. And Paris knew he couldn't get to Helen without help. We were the help, a means to his end.

HOMER

How did he pull off capturing Helen?

MUSE

After the takedown had been accomplished, Paris and his Archers were supposed to escape and evade, right? Ditch the vehicles. Sanitize everything. Link up and head back to the rendezvous point safe house. But they didn't.

HOMER

Were you initially aware that Paris' team had not returned?

MUSE

No, I wasn't immediately aware. I was still maintaining UAV coverage over Vehicles One and Two. Vehicle Three, with Menalaus, did follow the plan and returned to the safe house rendezvous point. From that standpoint, everything was going according to plan. But things quickly changed when Vehicle One, which was following Vehicle Two, headed through an intersection and was T-boned by a dump truck.

HOMER

Traffic trash? Coincidence?

MUSE

No way. We later discovered that Paris had hired the driver to crash into Vehicle One and to make the crash look like an accident.

HOMER

What did Vehicle Two do?

MUSE

Vehicle Two didn't stop. They had Helen and were under orders to get back to the safe house rendezvous point as quickly as possible. They radioed to us that Vehicle One was down, but that they were still on mission. The operators in Vehicle One were on their own.

HOMER

So now it was just Vehicle Two, followed by your UAVs overhead?

MUSE

Correct.

HOMER

Then what happened?

MUSE

The EMP.

HOMER

For the record, can you clarify what an EMP is?

MUSE

Sure. An EMP is an electromagnetic pulse or a transient electro-magnetic pulse, also known as a TED.

HOMER

What does an EMP or TED do?

MUSE

Both are brief bursts of electromagnetic energy, either natural or artificial. An EMP can be an electric field, a magnetic field, or an electromagnetic field. A lightning strike is technically an EMP, but one that can damage objects and kill people. In modern warfare, an EMP is used to knock out the computers running communications. In this case, an EMP knocked out my UAVs.

HOMER

Theoretically, a large enough EMP could take down the electrical grid of an entire country, correct?

MUSE

True, but Paris used a small EMP to take down my UAVs and disable Vehicle Two because modern vehicles have so many elec-tronics and computers. He killed all our communications. We were deaf, dumb, and blind. We had no idea what was happening.

HOMER

How did you ultimately find out what had happened?

MUSE

The information was pieced together from after-action reports and testimonies from the crews of Vehicle One and Two.

HOMER

Okay. Walk me through this next part. The EMP was triggered, disabling everything electronic or computer-controlled. Then what?

MUSE

Paris seized the initiative—took advantage of the chaos he created—and sent a vehicle full of his operators to assault Vehicle Two and take Helen.

HOMER

Any casualties?

MUSE

No. The crew of Vehicle Two was overwhelmed by speed, surprise, and violence of action. They got roughed up a bit but suffered only minor cuts and bruises.

HOMER

If Paris used an EMP, why didn't it take out his own vehicle?

MUSE

He was using an old vehicle with no computers or modern electronics. I don't know where he sourced the vehicle from, but it was a heads-up play on his part.

HOMER

So then Paris and his team grabbed Helen and exfiltrated with her, correct?

MUSE

Correct.

HOMER

How did the operators in Vehicle Two get out of the area?

MUSE

On foot. They fell back to the traffic crash site of Vehicle One. Once they had linked up, they all called for an extraction back to the safe house rendezvous point. They even took the truck driver who slammed into Vehicle One as a prisoner.

HOMER

Why take the driver?

MUSE

At that point, he was a potential source of intelligence.

HOMER

What happened once both elements from One and Two were back at the safe house?

MUSE

Everybody was debriefed. It's also important to remember who was there and who wasn't. I was on-site for the entirety of the operation with my team. Running both the UAV side and the TOC side, I basically served as the C-Two battlespace commander.

HOMER

To clarify, what is a TOC? And what is a C-Two?

MUSE

TOC stands for tactical operations center, and C-Two is command and control.

HOMER

Why were you serving in these roles?

MUSE

Because Menalaus was in the field with his element, and Paris was in the field with his. So, at the time of the initial operation, only Charon, my team, and I were on-site.

HOMER

Got it. Please continue.

MUSE

After what we thought was mission success, Menalaus and Vehicle Three made their way back, and Paris and his team were supposed to do the same. Menalaus and Vehicle Three arrived at the safe house after completing their post-mission surveillance detection route to ensure that they weren't followed. We thought Paris and his team were doing the same, but they never showed. And right when we noticed that none of his personnel had arrived, the EMP detonated, and Helen was snatched by Paris. After that, they scattered.

HOMER

So now it was just you, your team, Charon, Menalaus, and the crew of Vehicle Three at the safe house, correct?

MUSE

Yes.

HOMER

Can you describe the environment on-site?

MUSE

Controlled chaos. At first, we chalked up Vehicle One's accident to Murphy's Law. But when that EMP went off, we knew it wasn't a coincidence. A coordinated attack was at play. Initially, we didn't know who had attacked us, but we knew the original operation was compromised. Only when the Spartans from Vehicles One and Two, with the truck driver in tow, finally made their way back did we know that Paris had turned on us.

HOMER

What was the general reaction?

MUSE

Controlled chaos turned to all hell breaking loose.

HOMER

In what way?

MUSE

Well, for starters, the mission was completely blown. The whole premise revolved around Menalaus and Paris coming out from the shadows that their brothers had cast. Once out in the sun, so to speak, they were going to break away from their firms. They wanted to show their brothers and our community that they could stand on their own two feet without depending on their families for anything.

HOMER

And what better way to prove your worth than to pull off the biggest job in the history of private contracting, right?

MUSE

Right. But the truth of the matter was that Paris fucked over Menalaus. Paris could tell Hector and Priam that he acted because no one believed it was possible and because Hoplite's treatment of Priam deserved retribution, a mortal blow. But Menalaus now would have to go back to Agamemnon and say that he fucked up, that he thought he could handle it, but he couldn't, and that he would do his best to contain the embarrassment and fallout.

HOMER

Is it safe to say that Hoplite's reputation would take a huge blow because of Menalaus?

MUSE

Absolutely. This operation clearly showed that Menalaus would never, and could never, do anything without the support and guidance of his brother. Menalaus would have to beg for his brother's forgiveness and find some way to restore the honor of Hoplite.

HOMER

So, Menalaus' primary concern was honor? After everything you've told me so far, you expect me to believe that?

MUSE

Kind of. What Paris did couldn't go unanswered, or the story would ruin Hoplite forever. So, Menalaus knew he had to deliver a message of failure not only to his brother but also to Zeus.

Imagine that conversation. Menalaus had some thinking to do on how to spin this tale, and more importantly, who to spin it to first. Agamemnon or Zeus? Both bad choices. Both options were a no-win for Menalaus. But if he had any hope of salvaging something from this goat rope, he would have to reframe the story.

HOMER

What about Charon and Hades?

MUSE

Charon was bullshit. His job was to transport a person from Tartarus to Hades, a journey that turned said person into a shade. And come hell or high water, that's what he would do.

HOMER

So, what happened?

MUSE

Initially, we thought the truck driver was one of Paris' operatives and that maybe he had intelligence on where Paris was taking Helen. It was decided that Charon would take the driver.

HOMER

The driver got turned over to Charon?

MUSE

Somebody had to go. That's the deal when Charon gets involved. He collected his two coins, packaged up the truck driver, and ferried him off to Tartarus.

HOMER

Did anyone get any intel out of him?

MUSE

We found out later through back-channel sources that the truck driver was a nobody. He was just a down-on-his-luck guy that Paris found and paid in cash under the agreement that the guy would crash into Vehicle One.

HOMER

That's it?

MUSE

That's it. Wrong place. Wrong time. The driver wasn't a contractor, an operator, or a spy. He was just a regular guy. A patsy. A distraction. A way to create confusion while Paris absconded with Helen. I felt bad for that poor bastard. I still do.

HOMER

Who did Menalaus call first?

MUSE

His brother.

HOMER

Do you know what was said?

MUSE

Yeah, I do. I was there when Menalaus made the call.

HOMER

How did he spin the story? There's no way he told the whole truth.

MUSE

No, he didn't. He actually came up with a plausible version of the truth.

HOMER

Which was?

MUSE

He called Agamemnon and said that he had some news—that he'd heard, through the rumor mill, that an open contract had been placed on Helen Argos. He and his Spartans, who had just finished up a training contract, decided to look into the validity of the rumor and the feasibility of pulling off the job.

HOMER

So, what he said was basically true . . . from a certain point of view?

MUSE

Yeah. I guess everything can be true from a certain point of view, right? Anyway, I got the impression that Agamemnon was buying what his brother was selling, and he got even more excited when Menalaus reached the part about actually locating Helen and performing the interdiction stop to capture her.

HOMER

Wait a minute. Didn't you say that Agamemnon purposely excluded his brother from the original concept of operations meeting at Olympus?

MUSE

He did. But remember, that was before Trojan walked and Hoplite was the sole remaining party to the contract.

HOMER

So, Agamemnon didn't want his brother to embarrass him at the meeting with competitors present, but he'd be happy to have his brother complete the mission on Hoplight's behalf.

MUSE

Yes. If Menalaus captured Helen, Hoplite would win, and when Hoplite wins, Agamemnon wins. Honestly, I've never seen or heard the guy so happy. For a split second, he stopped being an arrogant prick.

HOMER

 Menalaus had a "but" coming. How'd that go?

MUSE

There's always a "but," right? Agamemnon went ballistic when Menalaus got to the part about Paris and his Archers ambushing his element and stealing Helen. He calmed down a little bit when Menalaus told him about the truck driver who got scooped up by his Spartans and how this driver was turned over to Charon to be taken to Tartarus and debriefed. Agamemnon made the decision, right then and there, that they—*we*—were going to get Helen Argos back at any cost, restore the honor and reputation of Hoplite, and destroy Priam and Trojan once and for all. He declared all-out war. Agamemnon promised to make me whole for my loss and hired me on the spot to provide intelligence, surveillance, and reconnaissance for him during his campaign against Trojan. He ordered Menalaus to sanitize the safe house and return to Hoplite headquarters for planning and preparation.

HOMER

In a nutshell, what did that planning and preparation entail?

MUSE

Agamemnon planned to call up all Hoplite affiliates to assist in the upcoming operation. In this exact moment, and as I mentioned earlier, Helen Argos became the face that launched a thousand drones.

ATTACHMENT 7

CASE NOTES: LAW ENFORCEMENT PRESS RELEASE

RELEVANT TEXT

FOR IMMEDIATE RELEASE

The Metropolitan Police Department is seeking the assistance of the public regarding information pertaining to a multi-vehicle traffic crash.

It is unknown if there were any injuries or casualties. No vehicle operators or passengers were on the scene when patrol officers arrived.

Anyone with information is urged to contact the Patrol Division Traffic Enforcement Unit.

CASE NOTES: LAW ENFORCEMENT PRESS RELEASE

RELEVANT TEXT

FOR IMMEDIATE RELEASE

The Metropolitan Police Department is seeking the assistance of the public regarding information about the possible abduction of a dump truck operator linked to the multi-vehicle crash mentioned in the previous press release.

The operator was not on the scene when patrol officers arrived.

The identity of the dump truck operator is not yet known. The Metropolitan Police Department is still attempting to obtain a positive identification.

Anyone with information is urged to call the Detective Bureau Missing Persons Desk.

SECTION 20

HOMER
Who notified Zeus?

MUSE
No one did. At least not right away.

HOMER
 Why?

MUSE
Honestly? I think that if Zeus found out what really happened, he probably would've just started raining down lightning bolts on everything and everyone associated with Hoplite, Trojan, and Helen Argos. And knowing him, he probably would've found some way to spin the situation to his advantage—rogue contractors and intelligence agents had plotted to overthrow him and take Olympus, so he had them all taken out in the name of national security. Something like that.

HOMER
So, Zeus was kept in the dark?

MUSE
Initially, yes. Agamemnon made a conscious decision based on the version of events that Menalaus spun him. He saw an opportunity to spin a story of his own and, in the process, dispose of a professional rival and former friend. By crushing Trojan and taking back Helen, Agamemnon would essentially win eternal favor with Zeus and lead the largest private army in the world.

HOMER

Greed and revenge. Do you think these were his primary motivators?

MUSE

Pretty much. Agamemnon developed the ruse, and he was the one who briefed Zeus.

HOMER

This is probably a rhetorical question, but what was Zeus' reaction?

MUSE

He was super fucking pissed—and that's an understatement. But Agamemnon, spinning his version of the truth, was able to talk Zeus down and lay out a plan to capture Helen and take Trojan off the board.

HOMER

What was his pitch?

MUSE

He sold his plan as a deep black, covert action that wouldn't blow back on Zeus at all.

HOMER

And Zeus signed off on this?

MUSE

When you think about it, Zeus was kinda backed into a corner. He really had no play. This plan was his only way out. Ultimately, he named Trojan, and everyone associated with the company, as an enemy of the state and authorized Agamemnon's covert action plan.

HOMER

What were the rules of engagement?

MUSE

Zeus told Agamemnon to act by any means necessary.

HOMER

By any means necessary? That completely blows my mind. What are your thoughts?

MUSE

Well, you'd think Zeus would want to keep things as tidy as possible. But because of Menalaus' lie to Agamemnon—and by extension Agamemnon's lie to Zeus—Zeus could now spin this mess to his advantage in multiple ways.

HOMER

How?

MUSE

Like I said before, this whole situation with Helen Argos began because Zeus couldn't keep it in his pants. So now, he could label Helen as a rogue intelligence operative who was collaborating with a rogue private military contracting firm. Both could then be declared terrorists, enemy combatants, or enemies of the state. Both posed a clear and present danger to the nation. Those threats needed to be mitigated. And all the while, Zeus could conceal his complicity and ignore the fact that his initial involvement with Helen was the catalyst for this whole mess. Once again, Zeus falls into a pile of shit and comes out smelling like roses.

HOMER

Switching gears; what was Priam's response when Paris showed up with Helen?

MUSE

I don't know.

HOMER

What do you mean you don't know?

MUSE

Priam didn't hire me.

HOMER

Then who did he use for ISR?

MUSE

Again, I don't know. Any disclosed information about what happened in the Trojan camp was either open-source or from various intelligence intercepts.

HOMER

Understood. Please continue.

MUSE

I'm speculating here. Priam probably could've turned Helen over, but in doing so, he would've been sacrificing his youngest son. And as pissed as Hector probably was at his brother, he wasn't about to send the kid to his death. Helen understood the situation and didn't want to leave, so she did whatever she could to stay alive and prove valuable to Trojan. They closed ranks and prepped for the war they knew was coming.

HOMER

Okay, so Priam was holding Helen while trying to come up with a plan. Do you know anything else about that period of time?

MUSE

Yeah. Something no one could've seen coming.

HOMER

What was that?

MUSE

Paris and Helen fell in love.

HOMER

Excuse me?

MUSE

Hey, life and death situations cause feelings to develop rather quickly. One thing that everyone overlooked, glossed over, or just plain ignored was that Paris had done early physical security and personal security work for Helen. Do you remember me telling you that?

HOMER

Yes.

MUSE

Well, apparently the benefits of that work were more than just monetary.

HOMER

Do you think rescuing her was part of his plan all along?

MUSE

Looking back on the situation now? Yeah, I do, but hindsight is always twenty-twenty.

HOMER

I'm just amazed.

MUSE

About what?

HOMER

This entire situation. And please, let me know if I'm way off base here. You have a woman seeking revenge against arguably the most powerful person on the planet. You also have a group of men who are brothers in arms and in blood who perfect the profession of private contracting. But a rift develops over the best way to sustain their creation, and that rift is widened by greed. That greed causes a tear that separates these brothers into two distinct groups—one that's ethically and morally sound, and another that's controlled from the top down to ensure that no matter what, the man on the top stays on the top. Then you have two brothers from these different sides who come together to get out from under the shadows they've been under their whole lives. They form a plan to take the woman who started this whole debacle, only to have one brother betray the other because of a secret love. This betrayal leads two powerful, dangerous, and greedy men to form a pact and start a covert war.

MUSE

You've got it right. But at the time, no one had any idea how that covert war would devolve.

HOMER

You mentioned earlier that Hoplite's business model ensured that if Agamemnon called on any affiliate, that affiliate was bound to answer, correct?

MUSE

Yes.

HOMER

But in this situation, you said that he didn't call on just one or two affiliates, did he?

MUSE

No, he didn't.

HOMER

How many did he call up?

MUSE

All of them.

HOMER

What can you tell me about the people who ran or were a part of these affiliates? Who was called first? How were the others recruited?

MUSE

Odysseus was called first. In my opinion, he was the most important asset that Agamemnon had at his disposal.

HOMER

What can you tell me about Odysseus?

SECTION 21

MUSE

What can I tell you about Odysseus? For starters, one of my intelligence sources I mentioned earlier, Dares Phrygian, says he's tough. But he's not just that. He's crafty, an eloquent speaker, and wise—Dares even described him as cheerful.

HOMER

What else?

MUSE

Bringing him on board wasn't easy. His contracting company, Ithaca, was doing very well. He was happily married to his wife, Penelope, and the last thing he wanted was to go on a campaign to clean up someone else's mess—especially Zeus'. Nevertheless, Agamemnon sent me, Menalaus, and another operative named Palamedes to get Odysseus to honor his obligation as an affiliate of Hoplite. I found out later that Odysseus had a premonition that if he went on this contract, he would be gone for a long time—like *lost*—on some kind of journey, despite what was promised to be a quick assignment.

HOMER

I'm not prepared at this point to debrief you on Wanderer. One special access operation at a time, understand?

MUSE

Understood. So anyway, Odysseus being Odysseus, he comes up with a plan to get out of going.

HOMER

How?

MUSE

By acting crazy.

HOMER

Excuse me?

MUSE

Yeah, crazy. Acting like a nut. Honestly, I don't blame him for trying to bail.

HOMER

Why?

MUSE

He lives on this nice ranch up in the mountains and is really into the whole old-school sustainable farming thing. He's got a good thing going, and word around the campfire is that he was looking to retire. So, the last thing he wanted was to go off on some bull-shit job from Agamemnon.

HOMER

So, what did he do?

MUSE

He hooked up his plow to an ox and a mule and was plowing a field when we got there.

HOMER

Okay. So what?

MUSE

The animals' strides aren't the same. He was plowing all over the place. And at the same time, he was sowing his field with salt and mumbling all kinds of crazy shit.

HOMER

Was his act convincing?

MUSE

I bought it. Menalaus bought it. We both thought he had finally gone insane; but Palamedes wasn't buying what Odysseus was selling.

HOMER

What did Palamedes do?

MUSE

He grabbed Odysseus' kid and thew him down in front of the animals and the plow.

HOMER

That was his idea to see if Odysseus was mentally sound?

MUSE

Yeah, and in a weirdly aggressive way, his idea made sense.

HOMER

How do you figure?

MUSE

If Odysseus was truly crazy, he'd just trample his kid and plow him under. But at the last moment, he veered away. His ruse failed, and he'd been exposed. Now he had no choice but to honor his obligation to Hoplite and Agamemnon.

HOMER

So, this Palamedes character actually pulled one over on Odysseus? That must be rare.

MUSE

He did, but Odysseus would have the last laugh. He never forgot or forgave Palamedes for what he did, and Odysseus got him back later on.

HOMER

What happened?

MUSE

The feud between Odysseus and Palamedes doesn't have any bearing on what happened, so I'll tell you now.

HOMER

Please. I'd appreciate it. I don't have much information on Palamedes, so every little bit helps.

MUSE

I can tell you that Palamedes was smart. He was an inventor. He was always tinkering with things, cobbling together equipment, and modifying weapon systems.

HOMER

Anything else?

MUSE

Like you said just a minute ago, he did something that not many people can say they've done—he outwitted Odysseus and essentially forced him to join the expedition against Trojan. He was smart. But he wasn't as smart as Odysseus.

HOMER

So how did Odysseus get his revenge?

MUSE

Not long after, Palamedes quickly saw that this covert war between Hoplite and Trojan was turning into a war of attrition and openly advocated for Hoplite to abort the mission and return home.

HOMER

That couldn't have gone over well.

MUSE

It didn't. Odysseus heard what he was saying and took in all of the information that he could. He then hid money in Palamedes' quarters and wrote a fake letter, purportedly from Priam, which promised Palamedes money if he'd turn on Hoplite.

HOMER

What happened to that letter?

MUSE

That forged letter found its way to Agamemnon, who ordered a search of Palamedes' living area. They found the hidden money placed by Odysseus.

HOMER

What happened to Palamedes?

MUSE

He was executed for treason. That entire ploy is just a small example of how cold-blooded and cunning Odysseus can be.

HOMER

What else can you tell me about Odysseus?

MUSE

Odysseus?

HOMER

Yes. Who is he? Where did he come from? What's his background? What's his personality? How does he think? To me, he seems pretty important, considering that he was recruited first. Clearly, he was a first-round draft pick. Teams usually succeed with a roster full of first-rounders.

MUSE

He's many things to many people. Some love him. Some hate him. He's a combination of a self-made man and a self-assured man. He's the living embodiment of the standards and codes of our way of life.

HOMER

How about his personality?

MUSE

He's self-confident but not arrogant. He's cunning and clever. He's not a liar, even though he will use trickery and deception to accomplish a task or complete a mission. He's a walking, talking contradiction. He's complicated.

HOMER

Complicated? In what way?

MUSE

He lives by his wits, as well as his weapons. He's an intellectual. He'll openly evaluate and analyze a situation and then demonstrate the logic behind his choices. He's a strategist and tactician. He's self-disciplined, but his curiosity gets him into trouble. He creates his own code of conduct through his actions. He's contemplative but capable of extreme violence that's almost on par with Achilles.

HOMER

Ah, Achilles. We'll come back to him. But hang on. This information is starting to blend together. Can you summarize for me?

MUSE

Sure. Simply put, there are some people you want in a spelling bee, and there are some people you want in a fight. I'd want Odysseus for both.

HOMER

You all have many spelling bees?

MUSE

I thought I was supposed to be the smart ass here. I'm trying to make a point, okay? You're the one who asked about him.

HOMER

Sorry. Please continue.

MUSE

Bottom line, and to sum up Odysseus, you'll find no better friend and no worse enemy.

HOMER

What can you tell me about where he came from? His background?

MUSE

All I know for sure is that he's a legacy admit from a premier intelligence agency's elite paramilitary unit. His father, Laertes, was a plank holder in the Argonaut program, and Odysseus followed in his footsteps. But prior to him being sheep-dipped into that paramilitary unit, Odysseus was a member of an intelligence support activity group in the military. I don't know the current code name for the group. They constantly change their name.

HOMER

Do you know what he did in that unit?

MUSE

His job in that group was to be the intelligence-gathering component for a joint special operations command. His focus was on collecting clandestine human intelligence and actionable intelligence before or during joint special operations missions.

HOMER

What else can you tell me?

MUSE

While he was with the group, he worked with Agamemnon, Menalaus, Nestor, and Priam when all those guys were running and gunning with top-tier units. At the time, they were performing the most complex, classified, and dangerous assignments out there.

HOMER

Anything else?

MUSE

Odysseus isn't just your stereotypical trigger puller, even though he can sling lead with the best of 'em. He's well-trained and well-versed in tactics, close-quarters combat, sniper and counter-sniper operations, and intelligence source development. The guy has worked, and still works, covert operations in permissive and non-permissive environments worldwide. He can speak several languages fluently. After working for that intelligence support activity group and doing paramilitary work, he retired.

HOMER

What did he do when he retired?

MUSE

He did what everyone else did. He joined the private contracting world and formed his own company, Ithaca.

HOMER

What does Ithaca specialize in?

MUSE

They basically do what I do, but their focus is more on the human intelligence and signals intelligence side of the house. They also do kinetic operations and wet work jobs, whereas I don't.

HOMER

What's your overall assessment of Odysseus?

MUSE

In my opinion, he's the best all-around operator under the Hoplite umbrella. Once he reluctantly joined Agamemnon's plan to take down Trojan and take back Helen, the other major players in Hoplite did too . . . well, most of them.

HOMER

Who were the other players?

MUSE

In addition to me, you had Agamemnon at the top. Then you had Nestor, Menalaus, Odysseus, Achilles, Diomedes, Big Ajax, Little Ajax, Antilochus, Automedon, Idomeneus, Kalchas, and Patroclus. Other minor operators and affiliates signed on, but these players were the most relevant. However, there's one person on that list who everyone knew they needed if they were going to win. Getting Odysseus on board was key because he had the best chance of recruiting the one person who hated Agamemnon most, the same person who had initially refused the call-up.

HOMER

Who was that?

MUSE

Achilles.

SECTION 22

HOMER

I know that from here on out, Achilles will be a frequent topic of discussion. I want to focus on his background and personality, just like we did with everyone else. Achilles is known to us, but no one could've predicted the pure, unbridled rage that he'd unleash, a rage that caused unprecedented levels of violence. I'm trying to figure out what made him tick and what happened to set him off. What can you tell me about him?

MUSE

One interesting thing is that Achilles' father, Peleus, was part of Argonaut with Odysseus' father, Laertes. Their fathers' connection explains their own connection and friendship. For this reason, Agamemnon needed Odysseus to join so Odysseus could recruit Achilles to the cause.

HOMER

That makes sense—appeal to their common bond. What happened during the recruitment process?

MUSE

Well, when the call-up came for all the Hoplite affiliates to muster, Achilles told Agamemnon to go fuck himself. Like I said before, nobody hated Agamemnon more than Achilles. So, when Achilles told the head of Hoplite to fuck himself, the prevailing fear at the time was that the other affiliates would do the same.

HOMER

Did any other affiliates refuse?

MUSE

Well, obviously Odysseus tried—he even acted like a nut to get out of going. But when his ruse fell apart, Odysseus reluctantly went and was tasked with being the one to bring Achilles aboard.

HOMER

Okay. But what am I missing about Achilles? What do I need to understand?

MUSE

What you have to understand about Achilles is that he was born and bred for war. From the moment of his birth, his destiny was preordained. He was going to be the greatest soldier and the greatest warrior the world has ever known.

HOMER

How so?

MUSE

Every stage of his life was overseen by experts in health, nutrition, and mental and physical development. His tutors were world-class scholars and killers. From age fourteen to eighteen, he lived with, trained with, and learned from the greatest master out there, Khiron.

HOMER

Wasn't Khiron also known for his skills in medicine, philosophy, art, and music, in addition to combat?

MUSE

That's him. He even saved Peleus' life. Naturally, Peleus brought his son to Khiron to be trained by the man who not only saved him but also taught him.

HOMER

What can you tell me about the time Khiron and Achilles spent together?

MUSE

For four years, Khiron pushed Achilles to his physical and mental limits. When Achilles left Khiron's tutelage, he was an expert not only in physical culture but also in the arts of combat medicine, strategy, tactics, singleton operations, and small-unit operations. Achilles could think, fight, move, shoot, and communicate with the best of them. For someone so young, he had no peers.

HOMER

What happened when he left Khiron?

MUSE

When Achilles left Khiron, he enlisted in the military and became an infantryman. He believed what he was taught—that to lead, one had to learn how to follow.

HOMER

Is it fair to say that Achilles was a lead-from-the-front kind of guy?

MUSE

That's a very accurate assessment of him. After his time in the infantry, Achilles began the selection process for his special operations career, where he excelled. He eventually successfully screened for a top-tier special missions unit and stayed there. He was promoted to troop commander before retiring and going into the private contracting business like the rest of his peer group.

HOMER

What do you know about his contracting group?

MUSE

His group was called the Myrmidons, made up of former tier-one unit operators. They've been nicknamed the Ant Men because they're a small, strong, and capable group that's fierce and intensely loyal to their leader. They've embraced their ant-like moniker and persona. They wear brown armor whenever they engage in overt operations, but rumor is that even their concealable armor is brown.

HOMER

Did Achilles and Agamemnon serve together?

MUSE

Yes. Achilles served under Agamemnon in that special missions unit, and that's where their hatred for each other began.

HOMER

It seems to me they have a lot in common. They're both highly skilled and ruthless men. But how would you describe their differences?

MUSE

The main difference is subtle but important. Agamemnon is a by-any-means-necessary-and-at-any-cost type of commander. Achilles was also a by-any-means-necessary leader, but he also subscribed to a theory that a famous general once voiced.

HOMER

What's that?

MUSE

That the object of war is not for you to die for your country, but to make the other bastard die for his. That's why Achilles pushed himself and his men so hard. He trained, shaped, and honed himself and those under his command to be that proverbial razor's edge at the tip of the spear. He made the Myrmidons the finest fighting force in the world. The only people who came close were Menalaus and his Spartans.

HOMER

Okay, so how did that make them so different from one another?

MUSE

The thing you need to keep in mind is that Agamemnon doesn't care how many men die. He only cares that he wins.

HOMER

Are you saying that Achilles didn't care as much about winning?

MUSE

No. I'm not saying that. Achilles wanted to win just as badly, but he knew the value of loyalty and of the lives of those serving under him. He knew that if he pissed away the lives of his men, he'd run out of men. And more importantly, no new men would join him. He would never ask his men to do something that he wouldn't or couldn't do. This trait alone was a major reason he accomplished seemingly impossible missions with his special unit under Agamemnon. He inflicted heavy losses on the enemy while personally sustaining little to no casualties.

HOMER

Interesting. Is there any truth to the rumor that Achilles had never been wounded? Or that he couldn't be wounded or killed? I'm not talking about cuts, scrapes, bumps, or bruises. Everyone gets those. I'm talking about an injury that would've landed him on a casualty report.

MUSE

I've heard the same rumor. The legend goes that when he was a baby, his parents baptized him in magical water from some mystical river and that he was invulnerable.

HOMER

So, his magic-river baptism, coupled with his extreme physical prowess and stellar mission success rate, created this image that he was a living god. And Achilles didn't attempt to correct that view of himself. So, with each operation completed, his legend grew?

MUSE

Correct.

HOMER

I'm sure Agamemnon wasn't a big fan of that. If they hated each other so much, then why did Achilles become a Hoplite affiliate? And why did Agamemnon allow him to join?

MUSE

Because as much as they hated to admit it, they needed one another. Their relationship was the textbook definition of a toxic relationship.

HOMER

Please explain.

MUSE

Well, if he had been able, Agamemnon would have had Achilles killed. But he knew that with Achilles off the table, everything would collapse. Agamemnon understood that where Achilles went, his fighting force would go.

HOMER

So, Agamemnon needed Achilles and his forces in order to win. That makes sense. But why would Achilles need Agamemnon?

MUSE

To win glory and victory, Achilles needed enemies to fight. Agamemnon had plenty of those. And though the men had very different motives, they would achieve the same goal.

HOMER

Immortality.

MUSE

Immortality. Think about it. Agamemnon would recapture Helen Argos. He would crush Trojan and defeat Priam—he does all these things, and Zeus would be in Agamemnon's debt forever. That's Agamemnon's version of immortality. Now, we get to Achilles. He would get to fight against the only person who may actually be as good as him, Hector. So, win or lose, Achilles would also achieve his version of immortality.

HOMER

So, the two of them needed each other, and they needed to work together to accomplish their individual goals.

MUSE

Correct. But, for that to happen, Agamemnon needed to recruit Achilles. So, he sent the only person Achilles would listen to—Odysseus.

SECTION 23

HOMER

So, I want to understand more about Achilles' recruitment. Because from everything you've told me, Achilles wasn't motivated by money. He was motivated by the fight itself, but he wouldn't fight for people he didn't respect. And while there was a time in the military when Achilles had to obey Agamemnon, in the private contracting world, he was no longer bound by the codes of military justice, customs, and courtesies of rank—as evidenced when he told Agamemnon to fuck off. But what about his obligation as an affiliate of Hoplite? How did he get around that clause without being excommunicated, sanctioned, or whatever you call it in your world?

MUSE

He found a loophole. The call-up didn't specify exactly how many assets needed to be sent—only that all *available* assets be sent.

HOMER

Clever. How many assets were "available" at the time of the call-up?

MUSE

So, after telling Agamemnon to fuck himself, Achilles sent one volunteer along with a handwritten note to Agamemnon explaining that since Agamemnon was only running one operation, he would only need one Myrmidon.

HOMER

So, he claimed that *one* operative was the only available asset on hand?

MUSE

Exactly.

HOMER

Smart. Achilles fulfilled his obligation through a technicality. That's brilliant. I'm sure no one saw that move coming, and I'm sure it pissed Agamemnon off. So how did Odysseus manage to get Achilles on board?

MUSE

Getting Achilles on board was a twofold problem. First, we had to find Achilles and the Myrmidons. Second, we had to convince Achilles to join the endeavor. Agamemnon tasked Odysseus and me to work on this problem.

HOMER

 What were your roles?

MUSE

My role was to use my extensive network of sources and platforms to find and fix Achilles' location. Odysseus' role was to actually go and attempt to recruit him face-to-face.

HOMER

What was step one?

MUSE

Finding him. And that proved to be simple.

HOMER

Step two?

MUSE

Recruiting him. That step turned out to be the complex part of the problem, a problem better suited for Odysseus than for me.

HOMER

Where did you ultimately track him to?

MUSE

He was on a foreign internal defense contract and conducting by-with-through operations for a friendly desert nation. The nation was facing a surge in violent, religious extremism.

HOMER

What exactly did that contract entail?

MUSE

Not only were Achilles and his Myrmidons training the host nation's special operations forces to defend their country from within, but they were also joining these forces on counter-terror and counterinsurgency operations.

HOMER

How could he operate in a country like the one you're describing? I'm assuming the majority of men there have olive skin, dark hair, and dark eyes. Achilles has reddish-blonde hair, and his eyes have been described as a green that's flecked with gold. Hell, our sources tell us that most, if not all, of his Myrmidons are also fair-haired with light eyes. How were they able to blend in?

MUSE

By hiding in plain sight.

HOMER

Okay, but how? Hair dye? Fake contact lenses? Spray tans to darken complexions?

MUSE

Even better. They dressed as women.

HOMER

As *women*? How do you hide a muscular male physique in women's clothing? Wouldn't they look like really jacked dudes dressed in drag?

MUSE

They wore burkas—full-length, head-to-toe, flowing burkas with meshed veils that completely hid their eyes and concealed their physiques. Once they put those burkas on, they just became part of the scenery.

HOMER

Correct me if I'm wrong, but in those countries, women can't go anywhere unless they're escorted by a male family member, right?

MUSE

That's true, but they had a workaround for that. They had the darker-skinned Myrmidons dress like males in that nation normally would. They acted as the escorts. Nothing looked out of the ordinary.

HOMER

All right. So, now you knew where Achilles and his team were, and you knew what their contract had them doing. You even figured out how they were operating in that particular ecosphere. But how did you actually find them? Especially if they were dressed as locals and completely melted into the background?

MUSE

Actually, that was easier than I thought it would be.

HOMER

In what way?

MUSE

We just followed the trail of bodies.

HOMER

Trail of bodies? Didn't you say earlier that their contract was for foreign internal defense and by-with-through counter-terror and counterinsurgency training? How, or *why*, did bodies come into play?

MUSE

Achilles and the Myrmidons were teaching the host nation's premier counter-terror unit how to find, fix, and finish high-value targets.

HOMER

Go on.

MUSE

Common teaching methodology in the tactical, military, and law enforcement world is "tell, show, do." This method hits on the three major adult learning modalities. First, they would tell their students how to find, fix, and finish a target in a classroom-based, lecture-style format. Second, they'd show the students how to actually find, fix, and finish a target. In this instance, Achilles and his team were showing the counter-terror unit how to accomplish this task using out-of-the-box thinking.

HOMER

You mean dressing like women to hide in plain sight?

MUSE

Exactly. And finally, the students would then do the entire task themselves. If they could execute the "do" part—in other words, they learned what they were taught—the contract would be fulfilled and completed. We got on their trail during the "show" phase when Achilles and his team were personally carrying out these hits. The bodies of high-value individuals started turning up in public spaces, markets, restaurants, tea houses, and even streets. We knew Achilles had been operating there, and we just needed to establish a pattern to predict where the next hit would go down. It was kinda like detective work, except we weren't trying to arrest anyone or even stop the kinetic problem-solving from taking place.

HOMER

And by kinetic problem-solving, you mean murder, right?

MUSE

Please don't try to claim the moral high ground here. Governments solve many of their problems kinetically. Besides, we don't always press triggers or drop bombs—sometimes we cut checks instead of throats to make a problem go away. It's the way the world works.

HOMER

I know how the world works.

MUSE

I still haven't figured out who exactly you are, Homer, or who exactly you work for. But if I were a betting man, I'd say you work for one of the premier three-letter agencies. Probably one that has a domestic and foreign mandate for not only law enforcement, but also for intelligence, counterintelligence, and counterterrorism. I'm sure you've done the same things that these men and women do, and I'm sure there've been times where the end justified the means—even more so if you could get a proxy to do your dirty work. So please don't wrap yourself in your flag and hoist your shield to say what you do is right and good, and what we do is wrong and bad.

HOMER

I'm not going to apologize for who I am, or what I do, or what I stand for. But there's a difference between you and me.

MUSE

Oh yeah? What's that?

HOMER

Due process of law. I have the ability to take someone's property from them, their freedom, and even their life–but I need legal, moral, and ethical justification to do so. I need sworn affidavits and warrants signed by judges. My use of force has to be reasonable, necessary, and proportional, and each choice should be in the furtherance of a lawful objective, not an economic or political one.

MUSE

So, because what we do is for profit and what Zeus does is for political power, we're automatically the bad guys?

HOMER

Yes. Yes, you are. As you said before: don't hate the player, hate the game. I get paid for what I do, too. I get paid by the people who make the rules, just like you. But you and your fellow contractors work in the shadows because the game makers don't want their orders to come to light. I may work in the shadows from time to time, but what I do has to come to light. Right, wrong, or neutral. And everything eventually comes out in a court of law.

MUSE

I think I know where you're going with this.

HOMER

I'm held accountable by those with no accountability. You contractors and operators are held to a standard of plausible deniability. My problem isn't with you, Muse, or necessarily with anyone involved in this operation. My problem is that this whole thing started at the top and must end at the top.

MUSE

That's very noble. Short-sighted. Maybe even a little naive. But still noble in your particular way. I guess I look at our roles like this: you and I are just different sides of the same coin. In the end, we all get spent.

HOMER

Maybe. Now, where were we?

MUSE

Following the trail that Achilles had left us.

HOMER

And where did that trail lead you?

MUSE

A pretty unlikely place, considering who we were trying to find.

HOMER

Where did you finally track him down?

MUSE

At an open-air farmer's market.

HOMER

You mean to tell me you found Achilles shopping at a local farmer's market?

MUSE

Not like one of those hipster ones, but a real one. It was certainly surprising, but that location was actually a brilliant tactical and strategic choice in committing to the whole hiding-in-plain-sight thing.

HOMER

How so?

MUSE

Think about it—Achilles and his Myrmidons were operating in a totally non-permissive environment and fully engaged in the "show" phase of their contract. They were teaching their students how to hunt down and either capture or kill a high-value target.

They had to fully embrace and commit to their role as women in this society. And in this culture that they were operating in, the women shop while their male escorts go to coffee shops, tea houses, or hookah bars to wait for their women.

HOMER

No resupply drops?

MUSE

Keep in mind, home for these operators wasn't on a military base. They were living and working out of local safehouses. And these safehouses didn't have maintenance or support staff doing the cooking, cleaning, and provisioning. All that stuff had to be done, or sourced, locally—and done in a manner that didn't look suspicious. Hence, Achilles and his men dressed in burkas for the daily shopping. This whole thing would have fallen apart in two seconds if you sent out muscular, light-haired, light-eyed, bearded dudes to get the groceries.

HOMER

You're right. That is brilliant.

MUSE

Another overlooked but equally brilliant component of the hiding-in-plain-sight plan was that Achilles, and his men could recon an area virtually undetected because of the mesh veil on their burkas. You could look anywhere, and no one would know where exactly you were looking or who you were looking at.

HOMER

It's definitely a good way to get eyes on a target.

MUSE

This wardrobe convenience, if you will, also explains the *modus operandi* of the find, fix, and finish taskings.

HOMER

Go on.

MUSE

We've established that a female in these countries can't be out alone without a male escorting her. And we've established that the darker-haired, darker-eyed members of Myrmidon who were acting as escorts would take their so-called women to the market to then sit and relax over coffee, tea, or a smoke?

HOMER

Yes.

MUSE

Well, the women in these situations aren't completely left alone. These open-air markets are surrounded by these coffee shops, tea houses, and smoke shops so the men can still technically watch their women while they shop but without having to follow them around. Make sense?

HOMER

I'm tracking.

MUSE

While the agents were shopping, they were also looking for targets. If a target was spotted, the women either radioed the target's location to their escort and the escort took down the target, or if the target was walking through the market, the women engaged the target.

HOMER

How were the targets taken down?

MUSE

Either with edged or stabbing weapons. Suppressed pistols or suppressed sub-guns were used sometimes, but these guns still made noise, so blades were preferred.

HOMER

What tactics were used in the takedowns?

MUSE

The most effective tactic was for the operators, still disguised as women and carrying goods, to approach the target while chatting. They would surround him, neutralize him in the scrum, and leave a crumpled, bloody mess in their wake as they disappeared into the crowded open-air market.

HOMER

So, you knew *how* they were operating. You knew *where* they were operating. You knew the *why* behind these operations. You knew that they would operate during the market's normal daytime business hours. You may not have known exactly *who* they were after, but you knew *what* they were after: high-value targets. How did you discover who Achilles and his Myrmidons were going after next?

MUSE

Odysseus called the host nation's national police and posed as a journalist. He claimed to be writing an article praising this nation's success in hunting down the country's most wanted criminals and terrorists. He simply inquired as to who remained a threat, and he asked for a copy of that list.

HOMER

And the police just gave the list to him?

MUSE

Sure did. The damn most wanted list was even posted on their webpage. Now we had confirmation of who had already been taken out and who was left on that list.

HOMER

Unbelievable.

MUSE

Never hurts to ask, right? The worst they could've said was no, and we still would've wound up with the list anyway.

HOMER

What did you do next?

MUSE

We took our lists and cross-referenced them with the known, dead targets and the locations where they were found. Then we researched the remaining names on the lists and their suspected locations—where they were believed to be and where they were known to frequently operate. From that cross-reference, we were able to roughly estimate where Achilles' next mission would be.

HOMER

Question. Were Achilles and his Myrmidons systematic? Were they moving from area to area in a methodical but predictable pattern?

MUSE

Like climbing the rungs on a ladder.

HOMER

If figuring out Achilles' next move was so easy, then why didn't the targets do something to throw him off, like changing locations or setting an ambush?

MUSE

Because Achilles had become a bad guy campfire story. An urban legend. The targets didn't do anything because no one thinks he'll be the next victim—it's always the other guy.

HOMER

Until you're the other guy.

MUSE

Truth.

HOMER

So, now you knew where Achilles could be found. What happened next?

MUSE

That next part of the plan relied on Odysseus finding a way to draw Achilles out.

ATTACHMENT 8

CASE NOTES: INTERNATIONAL PRINT MEDIA EXCERPT

RELEVANT TEXT

National Police authorities are baffled by a recent wave of unexplained murders that have taken place at several open-air markets across the country.

All of the deceased victims are reported to have been male and are believed to be between the ages of eighteen and forty years old. It is not known if the victims knew one another.

Authorities do not know if these murders are connected. The only similarities appear to be in the manner in which the victims were killed. Sources report that the vast majority of the victims were stabbed to death. A small number of the victims were reported to have been shot to death with small-caliber firearms.

National Police authorities are not calling these deaths the acts of a serial killer. They want to assure the public that the matter is being investigated at the highest possible level and that the public's safety is not at risk.

The Minister of Interior Security was reached for comment about recent reports that all the victims were on the county's most wanted list. The Minister stated that he could neither confirm nor deny the report's veracity but assured, "There is no cause for alarm. If these men no longer draw breath, then they can no longer draw blood."

SECTION 24

HOMER

What was Odysseus' plan to draw Achilles out?

MUSE

Since Achilles and his team were operating under deep cover, Odysseus figured that he'd also have to go under himself to make the approach.

HOMER

Dressed in a burka? Did that include you, too?

MUSE

No, and for a few reasons. One, a pair of single women would attract undue attention. Two, even if I was posing as the male escort, I'm not dark-complexioned enough to pass for a local. And even if I was, my training isn't in field operations. I wouldn't be much help if things went sideways.

HOMER

So, what did Odysseus come up with?

MUSE

We located the open-air market that Achilles and his Myrmidons would frequent to buy supplies, and Odysseus disguised himself as a shopkeeper and opened up a stall.

HOMER

What was he selling? Fruits? Vegetables? Meat?

MUSE

Nope. Weapons and gear.

HOMER

Really? What kind?

MUSE

Small arms mostly—rifles, pistols, knives. Body armor. Ammo. Helmets. Shit like that.

HOMER

He actually sold these things?

MUSE

Oh yeah. He even made some decent money while he waited for Achilles and his team to appear in the market.

HOMER

I still don't get how selling weapons and armor would draw Achilles out.

MUSE

Odysseus' stall would separate the wheat from the chaff, so to speak.

HOMER

How?

MUSE

Because the local women would walk right past Odysseus' booth and not even glance at his inventory. Men, however, would stop, look around, handle everything, admire, and haggle over prices. If a deal could be done, a sale would be made. Well, one day, a group of burka-clad women, shopping the market, walked by Odysseus' stall.

HOMER
And they stopped?

MUSE
They did. And one of the burka-wearing women seemed more interested in the weapons and armor than her companions.

HOMER
What happened?

MUSE
Discipline took over, and they all recovered their composure. They resumed their characters and moved on.

HOMER
So, no approach was made?

MUSE
Not that day, but Odysseus knew that they would be back to re-supply; so, the next time the women returned, he arranged with some locals to detonate a few flash bangs and pop off a few blanks to create some confusion and chaos in the market.

HOMER
And was Odysseus banking on Achilles and his men responding to the threat—not as regular civilians, but as trained soldiers preparing for an ambush?

MUSE
Correct.

HOMER

Did the plan work?

MUSE

It did. The second those flash bangs went off and those blanks were fired, Achilles gave a contact call, and all the burka-wearing women shed their robes, presented their weapons, and turned to address the threat while other members of the team took up three hundred sixty degrees of security. When no actual threat materialized, Achilles knew that the jig was up, and his cover was blown.

HOMER

What did Odysseus do?

MUSE

He shed his disguise and called me in with a large transport van to provide an extraction from the market. Then, he walked right up to Achilles, put his right hand out, and uttered an iconic line.

HOMER

What?

MUSE

"Come with me if you want to live."

HOMER

And did he?

MUSE

Yes. Achilles knew he was properly fucked; so, he and his compatriots all piled into the van, and we beat feet out of there.

HOMER

What about the Myrmidons who were posing as the escorts?

MUSE

They saw what went down and executed their own pre-planned escape protocols, along with running surveillance detection routes that would shake any tails and get them back to their safehouse.

HOMER

And that's where you and Odysseus went? Back to the Myrmidons safehouse?

MUSE

Yes. We went there to sanitize the place but also to wait for the rest of the team to roll in. Once everyone returned, we convoyed out of there and went to our safehouse to debrief. We explained why we were there and why we just fucked up their contract.

HOMER

Just as a side note, because I'm curious, how was the issue of the ganked contract handled? I'm sure the Myrmidons weren't too happy that they didn't complete the contract, and I'm sure the host nation footing the bill wasn't too pleased, either.

MUSE

Odysseus, being Odysseus, stepped in and called an audible.

HOMER

What was that?

MUSE

As a show of good faith with Achilles, he called the point of contact for the contract and explained that what had happened was actually pre-planned and part of the "show" phase. In other words, Achilles and his men were *showing* their students what to do if an operation was compromised.

HOMER

And the point of contact bought the story?

MUSE

Hook, line, and sinker. On top of that, Odysseus even proclaimed that the host nation's students were now ready to move on to the "do" phase, and that the students themselves could find, fix, and finish the remaining high-value targets on the list.

HOMER

Admirable. He went to bat for Achilles and his team?

MUSE

Odysseus even took it a step further. He declared that Myrmidon successfully completed the contract under time and under budget, and that the thriftiness entitled them to a bonus.

HOMER

So, not only did Odysseus smooth things over with the host nation, but he even managed to put some extra money in the pockets of Achilles and his team?

MUSE

Even further, he secured future training contracts for both Myrmidon and his own firm, Ithaca.

HOMER

That guy's something else, huh?

MUSE

It's amazing to watch him work. He never stops thinking or planning. His mind is as powerful a weapon as I've ever seen. He's a force multiplier, for sure.

HOMER

Okay. So, he secured some goodwill and smoothed things over with some extra dough, but how did he convince Achilles to join the cause? Technically, Achilles honored his obligation by sending one Myrmidon operator when Agamemnon called up the affiliates for assistance.

MUSE

Do you remember at the beginning of our debrief when I told you that Helen Argos used money, ideology, sex, and ego to exploit her targets?

HOMER

Yes.

MUSE

Well, Odysseus used the version of MICE with a *C* instead of an *S*.

HOMER

If I remember correctly, instead of sex, that means *compromise*.

MUSE

That's it.

HOMER

How did compromise come into play?

MUSE

Odysseus already got Myrmidon extra money. If Achilles were to balk at assisting the cause now, all Odysseus would have to do is dime Achilles and his team out to the host nation. Odysseus could easily make Achilles' team look guilty of cheating their contract and stealing the money. Their reputations in the contracting world would be ruined. Odysseus had Achilles there.

HOMER

Damn, that guy's good. Next?

MUSE

Odysseus then appealed to Achilles' warrior ideology and how this operation would be the fight of all fights. A full-blown covert war. I know it's an oxymoron, but he appealed to Achilles' live-to-fight and fight-to-live philosophy.

HOMER

Okay, but where's the compromise?

MUSE

Odysseus definitively compromised Achilles, and Achilles knew it. If word got out that Odysseus had tracked, located, and tricked the great Achilles into blowing a contract, then Achilles' reputation, along with his team's, would be garbage. Same result as the money angle. Odysseus had Achilles dead to rights on the M, the I, and the C. Which brings us to the E.

HOMER

Ego.

MUSE

Exactly. Odysseus laid it on thick but gave it to Achilles straight. He told Achilles that Hoplite couldn't win without him. He also told Achilles that he needed him to fight to end this covert war early—he was honest about wanting to go home and be with his wife and kid. He told Achilles that this conflict would be his last operation before retiring. But none of Odysseus' plans could happen unless Achilles fought.

HOMER

Was that enough to seal the deal?

MUSE

No. What closed the deal was when Odysseus told Achilles that fighting would be the biggest *fuck you* to Agamemnon, because after this war ended, everyone would know that Agamemnon was nothing without Achilles. Odysseus ended his pitch by assuring Achilles that he would win everlasting glory if he joined.

HOMER

And his pitch obviously worked.

MUSE

Sure did. Odysseus and Achilles cemented the deal with a handshake, and then we all traveled back to link-up with Hoplite to begin Operation Trojan War.

SECTION 25

HOMER

How long was Operation Trojan War supposed to last?

MUSE

This wasn't a breach, bang, and clear job. We needed to slowly infiltrate the surrounding area in and around Trojan's headquarters. We needed to set up safehouses, perform recon, run surveillance, and then start systematically eliminating targets until there was little to no resistance left. Once that was accomplished, we'd pinpoint Helen's location and go in, capture her, and extract her.

HOMER

Did the plan run as you envisioned?

MUSE

No. We ran into an unexpected problem.

HOMER

And what was that?

MUSE

Unbeknownst to us, Priam had allied with an organized crime syndicate known as the Sons of Apollo.

HOMER

No prior intel or indications about the Sons of Apollo?

MUSE

No. We should have foreseen this alliance because criminal

elements are often used to further the objectives of an entity at war. But we all assumed that this operation would be a straight-up fight between private military contractors. It wasn't. Especially when Agamemnon kidnapped the daughter of the Sons of Apollo leader.

HOMER

Why would he do that?

MUSE

To use her as a bargaining chip and mine her for any intel value.

HOMER

Did she actually possess any intelligence? Anything of value?

MUSE

Unknown. Her father, Chryses, offered Agamemnon a large sum of money in exchange for his daughter, but Agamemnon wanted more. He wanted the money *and* a guarantee that the Sons would stay out of the fight.

HOMER

How was that plan received?

MUSE

Not well. All the affiliate heads of Hoplite were in favor of turning the girl over for the money because the money could be used to help bankroll additional aspects of the operation. But Agamemnon wanted to have both the money and the non-participation guarantee. He didn't want to fight both Trojan and the Sons.

HOMER

So, what did he do?

MUSE

Against the advice of his affiliate heads, he made his offer to Chryses—pay the ransom for your kid, and you sit out the fight.

HOMER

Any counteroffer?

MUSE

Chryses responded that Agamemnon could pick one, not both. Agamemnon could take the money in exchange for the daughter, or, Agamemnon could return the daughter at no fee, and the Sons would guarantee no interference.

HOMER

What was the Hoplite response?

MUSE

Agamemnon refused and kept the girl hostage. He told the affiliate heads that Chryses would eventually come around, and they'd get everything they originally wanted.

HOMER

How did Chryses respond?

MUSE

The interesting thing about the Sons of Apollo is that, in addition to being an organized crime syndicate, they're also a pseudo-religious cult. So, Chryses prayed to Apollo for guidance and assistance. Legend has it that the answer came to Chryses in a dream. He claimed that Apollo came to him and told him to unleash a plague on Hoplite.

HOMER

A plague? Like a bioweapon?

MUSE

No. More like a cyberweapon. The Sons of Apollo used a cyber plague to infect and take down all of our computer systems.

HOMER

How long did this cyber plague last?

MUSE

Nine days. The attack was very sophisticated. Most people only envision the *bang, bang, shoot 'em up* aspect of organized crime without realizing that much of what these syndicates do is on the financial crime and cybercrime side of the house.

HOMER

Why do you think that is?

MUSE

Less risk. More reward. It's a pretty straightforward way of thinking. For what it's worth, I was personally impressed. The attack was on par with something I could do.

HOMER

Was this cyber plague like a large-scale ransomware attack?

MUSE

Pretty much. The terms were simple—Chryses gets his daughter back, and the plague gets lifted.

HOMER

What was Hoplite's response to the demand?

MUSE

Agamemnon still refused to hand the girl over. He actually wanted to implement a sort of scorched-earth policy.

HOMER

Scorched earth? What's that?

MUSE

Just start kicking in doors and shooting people in the face. But that approach was a non-starter. Even for Achilles.

HOMER

Really?

MUSE

Yes. An assembly with the affiliate heads was called to brainstorm solutions for this problem. The affiliate heads, especially Achilles, all agreed that the girl had to be returned to Chryses.

HOMER

What was their reasoning?

MUSE

Because Hoplite could in no way be tactically effective or efficient without our technology. There's no way I could. We needed to be back online.

HOMER

How did Agamemnon react after the war council?

MUSE

Agamemnon, facing all this pressure, realized that he had gone way over the tips of his skis by asking Chryses for both money and a non-participation agreement. He also knew that he'd lose the support of his men if he didn't do something to fix this problem that he created in the first place.

HOMER

Then what happened?

MUSE

You ever heard the saying, "Discretion is the better part of valor?"

HOMER

Yes.

MUSE

That's what happened here. Agamemnon agreed to return the girl and ordered Odysseus to personally take her back to Chryses. Once Odysseus returned the girl, the cyber plague was lifted, and Hoplite was back online. However, Odysseus also brought back a message from Chryses to Agamemnon.

HOMER

What was the message?

MUSE

FAFO.

HOMER

What's that stand for?

MUSE

Fuck Around and Find Out.

HOMER

That was the actual message?

MUSE

No, but it's pretty much what was conveyed. Hoplite made an enemy of the Sons of Apollo, and now the Sons fully supported Trojan. The Sons also said that they'd see Hoplite on the battle-field and then again in the afterlife.

HOMER

Chryses really referenced the afterlife? Or are you taking some artistic liberties?

MUSE

No, he actually talked about the afterlife. Remember, the Sons aren't straight-up criminals.

HOMER

I know. You said that they're a pseudo-religious group that's ex-treme in their beliefs.

MUSE

Yes, they're intense. And we weren't expecting this—having to fight a two-front war.

HOMER

How did Agamemnon receive that news from Chryses?

MUSE

Outwardly, he shrugged the message off. But deep down,

Agamemnon was pissed at Achilles.

HOMER

Why?

MUSE

Because Agamemnon thought for sure that Achilles, of all people, would've wholeheartedly embraced his open warfare strategy. Agamemnon felt undermined when Achilles was the voice of reason.

HOMER

That does seem pretty uncharacteristic for Achilles.

MUSE

Yes, in a way, but remember, Achilles doesn't like to take on casualties. Open warfare would have meant big losses on both sides.

HOMER

Good point. That doesn't sound like it would bode well for Agamemnon either.

MUSE

Yes, Agamemnon recognized that he caused the problem with the Sons and that open warfare would have been costly. But he was still angry. You have to remember, he's not used to having his orders questioned or undermined by someone he considers a subordinate. So, his response to Achilles' perceived transgression was to take Briseis as compensation.

HOMER

By *take*, do you mean physically capture? Like he did with Chryses' daughter?

MUSE

Yes.

HOMER

And who's Briseis? I've never heard of him before now.

MUSE

Her. Briseis was a deep-cover intelligence operative working for Myrmidon. She was rumored to be romantically involved with Achilles. And she was the solo Myrmidon operator that Achilles sent Agamemnon when all the affiliates were called up. Prior to the operation's official beginning, she was sent in to prepare the battlespace and study the atmospherics. She was also tasked with securing safe houses, ingress and egress routes, supplies, and logistics. She technically belonged to Achilles, but Agamemnon, as the overall commander, could acquire and use assets as he saw fit. Briseis was an asset he wanted for himself.

HOMER

Wanted her in what regard? Personally, or professionally?

MUSE

Both. Professionally, he wanted her for tactical, intelligence-gathering reasons. But personally, he wanted her so he could have leverage over Achilles.

HOMER

What did Achilles do when he found out about Briseis?

MUSE

Achilles wanted to pop smoke and leave. But he couldn't—he had made a promise to Odysseus. And if he left, his reputation would be tarnished. His name would be forgotten, and history would remember him in a disparaging light. So, Achilles decided to just sit it out until Hoplite was brought to the breaking point and Agamemnon was forced to remember that he needed Achilles to win.

HOMER

Quiet quitting?

MUSE

Essentially. I'm surprised you know the term.

HOMER

I'm old, but not that old. How was Achilles' decision to sit out received by the rest of Hoplite?

MUSE

Agamemnon brushed things off again and devised a plan to test Hoplite's resolve by attacking a Trojan target—he wanted to prove that Hoplite could win without Achilles.

HOMER

How did that sortie go?

MUSE

Awful. His plan backfired. The Hoplite element that went on the mission met heavy resistance. If Odysseus hadn't personally intervened, the whole attack would've been a rout. Operation Trojan War would've collapsed then and there.

HOMER

What did Odysseus do to prevent that rout?

MUSE

He launched a counterattack and laid down heavy cover fire that allowed the wounded to be evacuated. Once the wounded were clear, Odysseus led a rearguard action and ordered a tactical retreat back behind Hoplite lines.

HOMER

Was there an after-action debrief? And if so, how did it go?

MUSE

About as well as you'd expect. Probably worse, actually. One of the men who was on the mission, Thersites, openly voiced his anger about having to fight Agamemnon's personal war.

HOMER

What can you tell me about Thersites?

MUSE

He's vulgar. Obscene. Kinda dim-witted. Everyone was surprised when he was the one who stood up in the after-action and verbally attacked Agamemnon. He even called Agamemnon greedy and a coward.

HOMER

Greedy, I can understand. But why a coward?

MUSE

Because Agamemnon didn't go on the mission. He stayed back in the tactical operations center and directed things from there.

HOMER

What happened next? Agamemnon was clearly about to lose control.

MUSE

Odysseus knew that if Thersites' tirade was allowed to go on, the other affiliates would leave. Odysseus had to do something to win back Hoplite. So, against his better judgment, Odysseus stood up in the middle of the after-action and told Thersites to shut the fuck up and sit back down, or he was going to knock him on his ass.

HOMER

Did Thersites listen?

MUSE

No. And Odysseus followed through on his threat—cracked him right in the mouth and then followed up with a punch to the gut that doubled Thersites over.

HOMER

What happened next?

MUSE

Thersites picked himself up off of the ground, wiped the blood away from his mouth, sat back down, and shut up. That pretty much ended the let's-not-fight-Agamemnon's-war line of thought. But the seed of doubt was sown because Thersites simply said what everyone in that room was already thinking.

HOMER

Doubt and distrust can be a dangerous thing in tactical situations. How was this dealt with?

MUSE

Odysseus approached Agamemnon and asked permission to

personally plan and lead another operation against a different Trojan objective.

HOMER

Was he granted permission?

MUSE

He was.

HOMER

What happened next?

MUSE

Somehow, news of the upcoming Hoplite deployment reached Priam, and he ordered a sortie to counter the attack.

HOMER

What was that like?

MUSE

Try to picture two equally capable and equipped tactical elements maneuvering toward one another in an urban warfare setting—inching closer to each other in a lethal game of hide-and-seek. But just before both elements met, Paris offered to end hostilities by proposing to fight Menalaus.

HOMER

Like a duel? And this was Paris' idea?

MUSE

Yeah, like an old-school duel. And no, Hector devised the plan.

HOMER

Hector? Why?

MUSE

Hector never wanted any part of this fight, either. He just wanted to end things honorably and allow his brother to save face for what he'd done by running off with Helen.

HOMER

Even at the cost of his own brother's life?

MUSE

From what I heard, the decision was a hard one. But in the end, Paris had made this mess, and Hector wasn't about to throw other people's lives away to clean it up.

HOMER

So, was Menalaus on this particular mission?

MUSE

No. As I said earlier, Odysseus had command, but when Paris hacked our comms and offered to fight Menalaus, both sides halted and called a ceasefire while the message was relayed back to our tactical operations center.

HOMER

I'm assuming Menalaus accepted?

MUSE

Eagerly.

HOMER

What were the terms?

MUSE

Hand-to-hand combat. No firearms or other weapons would be allowed. Also, both parties agreed to stop combat while the duel took place, along with a promise to abide by the outcome. If Menalaus won, he got Helen back, and Hoplite would collect on the contract with Zeus. If Paris won, Helen would stay, and the contract with Zeus would go uncompleted and could not be reinitiated by Hoplite or any of its affiliates or members. Either way, the war would end.

HOMER

Did Paris ever stand a chance?

MUSE

No. He was beaten quickly, soundly, and badly. He needed to be rescued by Hector before Menalaus killed him.

HOMER

That's it? They fought, and Menalaus won. Was it really over that fast?

MUSE

What'd you expect?

HOMER

I don't know. Something more . . . epic?

MUSE

That shit only happens in the movies and video games. Their fight was as if a guy who only hits the heavy bag stepped into the ring with a professional boxer. Menalaus was just that much better than Paris at the close-quarters, combative stuff.

HOMER

I remember you saying that even though Paris didn't like hand-to-hand combat, he could hold his own.

MUSE

I did. And he can, but not when going up against someone like Menalaus.

HOMER

Okay, Menalaus won. Shouldn't the war have ended?

MUSE

It should've, but it didn't. A Trojan operator named Pandarus who was also one of Paris' Archers, shot and wounded Menalaus.

HOMER

So, Paris lost and got rescued by Hector, and Menalaus got shot. What happened next?

MUSE

Since the rules were broken and the fight's outcome wasn't honored, a battle between Hoplite and Trojan began immediately.

ATTACHMENT 9

CASE NOTES: LOCAL PRINT MEDIA EXCERPT

RELEVANT TEXT

A massive cyberattack that lasted nine days has mercifully ended.

The attack did not affect citizens' physical safety but did impact their digital well-being. An official speaking on the condition of anonymity indicated that the top priority for officials is getting everyone back online and limiting the e-damage caused by the attack.

This cyberattack reportedly took down all computers and IT systems over a large geographical area centered on the city's industrial section.

Authorities do not yet know who is behind this attack. To date, no one has claimed responsibility. Officials want to reassure the public that the investigation is ongoing, and anyone who has information is urged to contact federal authorities or the Metropolitan Police Department.

Those seeking to report specific information will be promised anonymity.

SECTION 26

HOMER

Okay, the battle between Hoplite and Trojan began. What happened next?

MUSE

Hoplite operator Diomedes personally killed or wounded a shit ton of Trojans, including Pandarus.

HOMER

Pandarus? The guy who shot Menalaus?

MUSE

That's him. Diomedes took him out.

HOMER

Did Diomedes engage with anyone else?

MUSE

He fought and beat one of Trojan's top operators, Aeneas.

HOMER

Did he kill him?

MUSE

No, but Aeneas had to be rescued by one of the Sons of Apollo, who then warned Diomedes not to war with them or Trojan, or Hoplite would suffer the consequences. But by that point, it was too late. The conflict had turned into a back-and-forth gun fight that ebbed and flowed like the tides.

Homer

Hoplite seemed to have the upper hand.

Muse

They did. The only thing that prevented a total Trojan defeat was Hector. He did what Odysseus had just recently done—Hector evacuated his men while under fire and safely got them back behind their lines to rest, rearm, and refit.

Homer

From what you're saying, Trojan took it on the chin, and had Hector not been around, Hoplite could've won the whole thing then and there. So, here's my question: how did Hector respond and rally his operators?

Muse

The following afternoon, Hector launched an assault on a Hoplite objective and got into a good one-on-one with Ajax.

Homer

Who won that fight?

Muse

It was a draw. Hector didn't think the operation would last more than a couple of hours, so he didn't bring any night vision capabilities to keep fighting in the dark. So, when night fell, both sides tactically withdrew for the night.

Homer

Was this the first time Trojan assaulted a Hoplite position?

Muse

Yes.

HOMER

What was the Hoplite response?

MUSE

The decision was made to fortify our positions. But something else very interesting came out of that assault.

HOMER

What?

MUSE

Intelligence sources within Trojan reported an internal debate about returning Helen Argos to Hoplite and ending the conflict.

HOMER

Do you have any more information about this debate?

MUSE

Apparently, Paris offered to pay a reverse ransom. I really can't think of a better word for it. The reverse ransom was supposed to compensate Hoplite for its losses and allow Paris to keep Helen. The offer was delivered to Agamemnon, who responded that he needed twenty-four hours to discuss the offer with his commanders.

HOMER

Was the twenty-four hours granted?

MUSE

Yes, it was.

HOMER

Was there any actual discussion with the Hoplite commanders about Paris' offer?

MUSE

No. Agamemnon already knew he would refuse the deal. He did meet with the affiliate heads but didn't even bring up Paris' offer.

HOMER

Then what were the twenty-four hours used for?

MUSE

To make plans and preparations. We needed the time to fortify our positions even more. We reinforced walls, constructed mantraps, placed anti-personnel and anti-intrusion devices, set booby traps—things like that.

HOMER

So, the next twenty-four hours came and went. What happened next?

MUSE

Not to overstate the obvious, but the situation on the ground for both sides was quickly becoming untenable. The scale of the combat had become so big that news of the fight made its way back to Olympus and Zeus himself.

HOMER

I was wondering when he found out. I want to explore a tangent here, something that's been nibbling at the back of my mind. Something I can't quite figure out.

MUSE

What's that?

HOMER

How was this war taking place in a large population center in a first-world nation, and no one was aware of the fighting?

MUSE

Because stuff like this happens every day the world over.

HOMER

What do you mean?

MUSE

Think about it. How many shootings, stabbings, fights, and drive-bys happen every day? How many times have you heard about gang or drug violence happening in the streets or schools? How many times do you hear about officer-involved shootings? And how many times do you think tactical teams are going out and serving warrants on a daily or nightly basis?

HOMER

Good point.

MUSE

This type of violence is so common that it's become background noise in our daily lives. We banked on anything kinetic simply blending into everyday urban crime.

HOMER

Did it?

MUSE

At first. Unfortunately, we couldn't maintain discretion for long. Both sides went loud. And as I said before, that loudness made its way all the way to Zeus, who then issued a back-channel proclamation through proxies to both Hoplite and Trojan. He wanted the conflict settled once and for all.

HOMER

Were any other decrees issued?

MUSE

He went a step further and arranged for a full-scale press blackout that included traditional media and social media. He even ordered all local, county, state, and federal law enforcement agencies to stand down and let us fight it out. Zeus made it clear that from here on out, there would be no interference or assistance from anyone. We were now operating in plain sight with a mandate from on high to finish the fight. Time wasn't on our side, and certainly not on Trojan's either. Fighting began almost immediately.

HOMER

How did the conflict unfold?

MUSE

Trojan attacked and pushed us to our emergency fallback position. The only thing that saved us was nightfall.

HOMER

Trojan didn't have night vision?

MUSE

They did, but they didn't want to push their luck. They had us pinned down. We weren't going anywhere, so they camped in the neighboring buildings and alleys and made preparations to attack us again at first light.

HOMER

What was that like? Being essentially trapped?

MUSE

Creepy as hell. And Trojan started fucking with us psychologically by lighting small, controlled fires to make us think they were occupying multiple surrounding positions. They lit the area like stars in the night sky.

HOMER

What was Hoplite's response?

MUSE

First off, Agamemnon actually admitted his mistake in trying to isolate and marginalize Achilles by taking Briseis from him. Now, he didn't go to Achilles and say, "I'm sorry, please come back." But he did send Odysseus and Ajax on his behalf to apologize and request that Achilles rejoin the fight. If Achilles didn't join, there was a good chance that Hoplite would be wiped out and that many good people would die.

HOMER

Let me get this straight. Agamemnon admitted that he was wrong but still couldn't bring himself to meet Achilles personally?

MUSE

Yeah. Pretty much.

HOMER

What did Achilles say to Odysseus and Ajax?

MUSE

He told them that Agamemnon could fuck off again and that the only way he'd ever consider getting back in the fight was if Trojan breached their defenses and threatened to destroy Hoplite's safe houses.

HOMER

Why do you think Achilles drew that line in the sand?

MUSE

Because an attack on the safe houses would directly threaten Achilles, and he would then be acting in defense of himself and his men, not for Agamemnon.

HOMER

So, Odysseus and Ajax returned to Agamemnon and delivered Achilles' message, right? I know I keep asking a variation of the same question, but I can't imagine the message was well-received. Things weren't looking too great for Hoplite, so what was the response?

MUSE

If they couldn't get Achilles back in, Hoplight needed a different tactic. Odysseus grabbed Diomedes, and the two of them formed a two-man hunter-killer team. They went on a night operation and infiltrated deep into Trojan territory for the sole purpose of creating havoc at the listening and observation posts. They wanted to silently eliminate as many Trojan operators as possible. Think of this infiltration as a sort of psychologically intimidating and demoralizing action.

HOMER

Explain.

MUSE

Picture two highly trained, highly skilled, and absolutely deadly operators stalking their opponents in the dark. Striking from the shadows and then melting back into the darkness, methodically and mercilessly picking off people one by one.

HOMER

Okay. Can you describe the purpose of this attack?

MUSE

What they were doing had a similar psychological impact as a sniper on the battlefield. He or she creates fear and anxiety. Fear and anxiety cause your opponent to lose focus and maybe even interest in the task at hand because they're too worried that they will be the next victim of these death dealers.

HOMER

In your opinion, who would you say was the highest-value target Odysseus and Diomedes eliminated that night?

MUSE

Dolon.

HOMER

What can you tell me about him?

MUSE

He was Trojan's best scout sniper. He was a singleton operator, meaning that he alone went out on operations to recon, gather intelligence, and kinetically solve problems. He was stealthy but fast. Had incredible endurance, stamina, and patience. He was smart, athletic, and gifted with amazing accuracy and an uncanny ability to camouflage. Our intelligence sources and signal interceptions indicated that Hector asked for volunteers to go out and spy on our position to see how well-guarded and fortified we were. He wanted to see if he could exploit any of our weaknesses. Dolon raised his hand and volunteered. I don't think he knew that Odysseus and Diomedes were actively stalking the battle space. Dolon's primary mission tasking was to observe, report, and only use lethal force when and if targets presented themselves—but only as a secondary mission.

HOMER

Understood.

MUSE

By chance, Odysseus and Diomedes spotted Dolon. They saw the route he was taking, so they hid themselves among some of the bodies of previously killed Trojan operators and waited.

HOMER

Okay, then what?

MUSE

When Dolon stalked past their position, they jumped out and captured him. They dragged him to an abandoned structure that they had cleared earlier and tactically questioned him for intelligence.

HOMER

Tactically questioned?

MUSE

Yeah. Enhanced interrogation techniques.

HOMER

Enhanced interrogation techniques? You mean torture?

MUSE

You can call it whatever you want, but Dolon didn't respond to the questioning and refused to talk. Odysseus decapitated him and mounted his head on a piece of rebar. Odysseus then positioned the body so Dolon's head would be easily seen by Trojan forces in the morning. That was their last kill of the night. Odysseus and Diomedes made their way back to our position and secured from their mission.

HOMER

What happened in the morning?

MUSE

Trojan woke to find their listening and observation posts empty, along with the personnel assigned to those posts dead. They found Dolon's body and head. That level of violence and savagery wouldn't go unanswered. Hector immediately launched an assault on our main position. The fighting was fierce and bloody.

HOMER

Casualties?

MUSE

Agamemnon, Diomedes, and Odysseus were all wounded.

HOMER

Achilles?

MUSE

Still sitting out. He was holed up in his team's safehouse and never acted or attempted to mount an assisting effort to help repel the attack. Achilles did send Patroclus to check our casualty report. While at our tactical operations center, Patroclus received a briefing from Nestor, who urged him to convince Achilles to fight because good people were dying while he was riding the pine.

HOMER

What did Patroclus do?

MUSE

Nestor's speech moved him. He returned to the Myrmidon safehouse and begged Achilles to allow him to take Myrmidon assets. Patroclus wanted to help defend Hoplite's positions.

HOMER

Did Achilles allow Myrmidon to go?

MUSE

Yes and no. And this next part may be something you're interested in. According to my sources, there was some subterfuge—Achilles lent Patroclus his armor to try to fool Trojan into thinking that Achilles himself was leading the defense and anticipated counterattack. But Achilles issued a strict order to Patroclus.

HOMER

What was the order?

MUSE

Patroclus was only to assist with the defense and, if possible, to mount a counterattack, but only to the point of Trojan's retreat. Patroclus was not to pursue or rout them.

HOMER

Why?

MUSE

Because if Achilles rejoined the fight, he wanted the glory of being the one who defeated Trojan. He didn't want to share that glory with anyone else.

HOMER

Interesting. What can you tell me about Patroclus?

MUSE

He was a childhood friend of Achilles. They were both in the military, but Patroclus served in a special operations forces support element. He left the military around the same time Achilles did and followed Achilles when Myrmidon was created. Patroclus ran logistics and support for Myrmidon, but deep down, always wanted to be a shooter. So, to reward his friend's loyalty, Achilles took a page out of Priam's playbook. He trained up Patroclus similarly to how Priam trained up his sons. Rumor has it that Achilles, upon his death or retirement, was grooming Patroclus to take over Myrmidon.

HOMER

Can you describe Patroclus for me?

MUSE

Dares Phrygian, the intelligence source I mentioned earlier, described him as being handsome and powerfully built with gray eyes. From my interactions with Patroclus, I'd say he was modest and dependable. Wise beyond his years. He was almost the opposite of Achilles. He was a very capable operator, but he was kinder and more compassionate than Achilles.

HOMER

Got it. So, while this scheme played out, with Patroclus helping defend Hoplite's positions, what was Trojan doing?

MUSE

Hector was leading the assault on our main position. Our operators defending the main gate were overrun and killed to the last man. The gate was breached, and Hector led his forces into our inner courtyard, which served as our muster point. This area was located just past the main gate.

HOMER

Can you describe the combat?

MUSE

The fighting was brutal. Close quarters, contact distance, bloody. There were so many dead and dying on both sides that I was horrified, even watching from my drone and camera feeds. I can't even imagine what it must've been like on the ground.

HOMER

Maybe you can answer a question for me on this subject. From what I've pieced together from communication intercepts, one of Hector's team or element leaders, Polydamas, appeared to urge Hector to fall back. Supposedly, Polydamas felt like they were pushing their luck or felt like they were getting sucked into something. But Hector ignored the request. Is there any truth to that rumor?

MUSE

I don't know. But I can tell you that Hector most certainly did not fall back or ease the pressure he was putting on Hoplite. If anything, he pressed harder. As time went on, more and more Hoplite operators fell.

HOMER

Any reinforcements?

MUSE

None. By this point in the battle, the Sons of Apollo joined the fight, and with their help, Trojan breached the door to our inner compound building and began a room-to-room, floor-to-floor clearing operation. They were fighting their way to our tactical operations center.

HOMER

And still no reinforcements?

MUSE

From whom? We had no one left to call. We had no idea that Patroclus, wearing Achilles' armor, was maneuvering Myrmidon to our defense.

HOMER

His arrival must've been an enormous morale boost.

MUSE

It was. But remember, we all thought he was Achilles and Trojan did too, because their attack stalled and collapsed under the Myrmidon assault. Hector recognized what his forces were up against now that they had lost the initiative. Hector was left with no choice—he ordered a tactical withdrawal.

HOMER

Did that end the fighting for the day?

MUSE

It should've, but it didn't. Patroclus ignored orders and decided to pursue.

HOMER

He disobeyed a direct order from Achilles?

MUSE

Under his command, Patroclus and Myrmidon fought Hector and his forces all the way back to the gates of the Trojan compound. But waiting there were additional elements of the Sons of Apollo. The Sons waited for Patroclus and Myrmidon to pass by before ambushing from the rear.

HOMER

So now Patroclus and Myrmidon were caught between Trojan and the Sons?

MUSE

Correct. Both forces attacked, and Patroclus was killed by Hector.

HOMER

But Hector thought he killed Achilles?

MUSE

He did. Hector didn't realize the ruse until he stripped the body armor, ballistic helmet, and ballistic face mask from the body. Only then did he realize that he hadn't been fighting Achilles.

HOMER

But even having Achilles' armor would've been a huge victory for Trojan and demoralizing for Hoplite, correct?

MUSE

Yes. Having the armor was one thing, but letting Trojan get Patroclus' body would have been an even bigger deal. So, an effort was made to retrieve his body from the field.

HOMER

Leave no man behind?

MUSE

Leave no man behind. It's not just a saying with these guys.

HOMER

What can you tell me about Achilles' reaction to Patroclus' death?

MUSE

He was devastated, but at the same time, he became extremely focused and turned that anger and rage toward Trojan and Hector.

HOMER

He had no armor. There's no way Achilles would handicap himself like that.

MUSE

Well, he did. He just put on his battle belt, sheathed his knife, press-checked and holstered his pistol, grabbed a spare chest rig, loaded it up with spare magazines, picked up his rifle, press-checked that, and left to recover his friend's body.

HOMER

What was that like?

MUSE

I'll tell you what I saw from watching my drone feeds of Achilles. His work was beautiful and terrifying at the same time. I couldn't imagine what being on the receiving end of his rage looked like.

HOMER

What was the Trojan reaction to the actual Achilles' appearance in the battlespace?

MUSE

Shock and awe is overused, but the phrase applies here. His appearance also created a tactical pause, or lull, in the fighting. Enough that Hoplite forces were able to fight their way to Patroclus and carry him away. Once Patroclus was back behind friendly lines, both sides broke contact and ended the fighting for the night. Both Hoplite and Trojan could rest, rearm, refit, and tend to their wounded and dead.

HOMER

What did Achilles and Myrmidon do?

MUSE

They mourned their fallen brother and prepared for the next operation.

HOMER

In your opinion, would you consider this skirmish a Trojan or Hoplite victory?

MUSE

Six one way, half a dozen the other. Trojan could claim a minor victory in that they stole Achilles' armor. And I'm sure the armor would look really cool hanging in some team room somewhere, but ultimately, Trojan couldn't finish the job. Likewise, Hoplite could claim a minor victory because Achilles joined the fight, but at the cost of his best friend's life and his armor.

HOMER

So, for the rest of the conflict, did Achilles wear Patroclus' armor?

MUSE

No, they weren't the same size. The Hoplite armorer Hephaestus made Achilles a new set of armor, including plates, plate carrier, ballistic helmet, and face mask. The whole nine yards.

HOMER

Okay, so both sides rested, rearmed, and refitted. What happened next?

MUSE

In the morning, Agamemnon personally went to Achilles, offered him a shit ton of money, and ordered that Briseis be reassigned back to Achilles and Myrmidon. But Achilles was indifferent. At a loss, Agamemnon asked Achilles what he wanted and how he could make it up to him.

HOMER

What was Achilles' answer?

MUSE

Achilles answered that he wanted to be turned loose and supported while he and his Myrmidons went to work.

HOMER

Did Agamemnon agree to these terms?

MUSE

He did. And Hoplite prepared for the fight.

ATTACHMENT 10

CASE NOTES: GOVERNMENT PRESS RELEASE

RELEVANT TEXT

FOR IMMEDIATE RELEASE

In partnership with local, county, and state emergency services, your federal government will conduct large-scale, live fire training exercises in the city's industrial section.

These exercises are part of an ongoing effort to train our first responders in how to respond to large-scale, mass-casualty, and terroristic events.

Civilians, the media, and unauthorized personnel are discouraged and prohibited from entering the designated training area(s).

The safety of the public is our primary concern. Please know that normal law enforcement, fire, and emergency medical services will be in place.

Your federal government would like to take this opportunity to thank all of our involved partners, as well as those impacted by this training exercise, for their cooperation, understanding, flexibility, and patience.

Please note that if you see something that you consider separate from this training exercise, immediately call federal authorities or the Metropolitan Police Department.

SECTION 27

HOMER

How did Achilles prepare for this operation? This fight? What's that process like for someone like him?

MUSE

He fasted, meditated, and prepped his gear. And when the time came to launch the assault, he led his people out. His assault was nothing but pure rage and focused aggression as he started absolutely slaughtering Trojans.

HOMER

What type of tactics?

MUSE

Nothing fancy. And I think that surprises people who aren't in this world or don't work in a career that requires you to be armed. These guys do the fundamentals better than anyone else.

HOMER

Can you provide an example of these fundamentals?

MUSE

Sure. Hoplite elements established a base of fire, and Myrmidon was the maneuver element. As they cleared an area by fire, they would lift, shift, and do it all over again.

HOMER

Any other tactics implemented?

MUSE

Another example is the skirmish line, something only used when the terrain allowed it. Hoplite would simply form a line and clear that area by fire as well. They literally drove the Trojans back, and all Hector could do was fight a defensive rearguard action.

HOMER

Can that rearguard action be fought indefinitely?

MUSE

No. It's a defensive action, and at some point in the fight, Achilles and his team cut the Trojan force in half near the river and decimated them. Hoplite operators were dropping so many bodies, the river seemed to fill up with the dead and dying. The water even turned red.

HOMER

Where was Hector? Was he with the element trapped by the river?

MUSE

No. Hector was with the other half, but Achilles didn't know that. He was in this berserker mode, and his only goal was to slaughter his enemies to the last man. Once that was done, Achilles would turn his attention to the remaining half and do the same. He was so focused on killing every last Trojan that he personally engaged in a foot pursuit of a singleton operator who was running away. I tasked my UAVs to track both Achilles and Myrmidon while they were in the field.

HOMER

So, you had eyes on Achilles the whole time?

MUSE

Yeah. I had eyes on everything going on in the AO.

HOMER

AO?

MUSE

Area of operation.

HOMER

So, when Achilles went off on his foot pursuit, what happened to the force that Myrmidon was in contact with?

MUSE

When Achilles went after the singleton, the fighting on that part of the battlefield paused. Their commander was chasing down a squirter—not something that's normally done.

HOMER

Did Achilles catch him?

MUSE

Yes. He caught him and killed him. But that lull in combat allowed the element under Hector's command to break contact, get back behind their lines, and barricade themselves in a fortified safehouse. Hector prepared to mount a last-ditch defensive effort.

HOMER

What happened to the element that was cut off and engaged with Myrmidon?

MUSE

All killed.

HOMER

What happened next?

MUSE

Like I said before, our intelligence sources and my UAV feeds revealed that the remaining Trojan elements retreated into their fortified safehouse, except for Hector, who remained outside the gated entry to their compound.

HOMER

Why do you think he remained outside?

MUSE

I honestly believe he stayed out of a sense of duty and honor. Maybe a sense of shame at having been routed. Deep down, he believed it was his duty to defend his family's legacy and shield his father and brother from the inevitable if Hoplite broke through. So, he stood his ground and faced Achilles one-on-one.

HOMER

One-on-one?

MUSE

Yeah. They squared off with one another, like a showdown.

HOMER

Why? Why didn't Achilles or any of his operators just gun Hector down? Why take the chance in a face-to-face fight?

MUSE

Revenge. Anger. Rage. Ego—take your pick. Achilles held his men back and went to fight Hector by himself so that he could personally kill the man who killed his friend. Achilles also wanted to be the man who took down the great Hector and, as a result, earn his place in history as the world's greatest warrior in the age of modern warfare.

HOMER

So, no one else would take credit for that kill but Achilles?

MUSE

Correct. He was going to kill Hector or die trying. I'm sure Hector was thinking the same thing—kill Achilles or die trying. One would live, and one would die. Either way, the war would end for one of them that day.

HOMER

Okay, so Achilles held his forces back and approached Hector. Then what?

MUSE

Achilles made it a point to take his ballistic helmet and face mask off so Hector could see who he was fighting this time. Hector did the same.

HOMER

Then what?

MUSE

This whole debrief is about setting the record straight on what actually went down, right?

HOMER

Yes.

MUSE

Well, there's this misremembering about how their fight went. Achilles versus Hector has become something of an urban legend, claiming the fight was some epic blow-for-blow, toe-to-toe, knock-down, drag-out slugfest. Hell, there's so many "So no shit, there I was" accounts that if each testimony of the fight were true, you could easily fill a hundred-thousand-seat stadium with so-called witnesses. The more times this story is told, the more exaggerated, bloody, and heroic it becomes.

HOMER

Then what was the fight really like?

MUSE

From my vantage point—watching the feeds from my UAVs and UGVs—this fight was like most fights and combat situations. The result was close. Movements were fast. It was violent. Are you familiar with the Rule of Three?

HOMER

I am. But for the record, can you please explain the concept?

MUSE

Sure. The Rule of Three was created by a certain federal, three-letter law enforcement agency that studied the data from thousands of gunfights. The data showed that the vast majority of these fights had three constants.

HOMER

And those constants were?

MUSE

One, the average gunfight lasts approximately three seconds. Two, the average distance between opponents is approximately three feet. Three, the average number of rounds fired is three.

HOMER

And that's what happened here?

MUSE

Yes. The conflict was over in exactly three seconds. Achilles and Hector were never more than three feet apart, and between the two of them, three rounds were exchanged.

HOMER

And you captured this footage on your drone feeds?

MUSE

I did. And this fight also followed another truism of combat.

HOMER

Which is?

MUSE

Speed, surprise, and violence of action—another three constants.

HOMER

How did it go down, then?

MUSE

Hector actually got the first round off and took Achilles by surprise. I honestly think Achilles thought Hector would go for his rifle because it was slung across his chest. But Hector dropped his right hand from the grip of his rifle to his pistol, and as he presented his weapon, he dropped his left hand from the fore-grip on his rifle and let it hang from its sling. Once he drew his pistol—and the pistol was at eye level—Hector fired one round.

HOMER

Did that round hit Achilles?

MUSE

Center mass. Right in his plate carrier.

HOMER

Did Achilles give any indication that he'd been shot?

MUSE

You can tell by the video feed that the shot certainly surprised him, but it didn't stagger him. Achilles instantly responded by lifting his rifle and firing two rounds.

HOMER

Was Hector hit by any of those rounds?

MUSE

Both hit. The first round hit him center mass in his plate carrier.

HOMER

And the second round?

MUSE

Right in the neck. And when he got hit, Hector dropped his pistol, grabbed his throat, and then slowly collapsed to the ground.

HOMER

Then what?

MUSE

Achilles walked right up on him. I thought he was going to deliver a make-sure round, but he didn't. Achilles knelt down next to Hector and stayed with him until he died.

HOMER

Do you know if any words were exchanged between the two of them?

MUSE

One of the Myrmidons, who was close to the fight, told me later that he could hear Hector gargle out something to the effect that Achilles would die in this war, too.

HOMER

Do you know if Achilles said anything back?

MUSE

That same operator said he heard Achilles say, "My fate has found me. When I die, let it be with honor like you."

HOMER

And then what?

MUSE

Hector died, and let me tell you . . . have you ever heard someone describe silence as deafening?

HOMER

Yes.

MUSE

When I tell you that the silence immediately following Hector's death was deafening, I mean deafening in the strictest possible sense. There was no radio chatter at all over the net, ours or theirs. The air was heavy with stunned disbelief and a shared sense of "Now what?" radiating from both sides.

HOMER

You seem like you have something else you want to say.

MUSE

I'm only stating my opinion here, but I honestly believe that most people in Hoplite and Trojan thought that if these two men met on the battlefield, they both would've killed each other.

HOMER

Like some sort of mutually assured destruction?

MUSE

Yeah.

HOMER

What else happened? What else did you see from your video feeds?

MUSE

Nothing—no movement from either side. From the feed, I watched Achilles get up and stand over Hector's body in the middle of a street, with a congregation of Hoplite operators on one side and Trojan operators on the other. The stillness and silence hanging in the air were both surreal and eerie.

HOMER

I want to talk about what happened next because what we've been able to piece together shocked us all. I can only imagine what it must've been like for you and everyone else on the scene. Can you speak to that event?

MUSE

You're right. The scene was shocking. But it's important to remember that two events took place that day. All anyone remembers is the second.

HOMER

Fair enough. Please tell me about the first event.

MUSE

We fully expected an immediate reaction from Trojan. We expected them to mount a full-scale assault, break out from their compound, and retrieve Hector's body from the battlefield. What we didn't expect was that only one man would come out and confront Achilles.

HOMER

Our sources indicated that one person was Paris.

MUSE

Your sources are wrong. Paris didn't fare too well when he tried to fight Menalaus, and he would have fared worse going up against Achilles.

HOMER

Then who did confront Achilles?

MUSE

Priam.

SECTION 28

HOMER

Priam? The head of Trojan? Hector's father? He came out alone to face Achilles?

MUSE

Yeah. We couldn't believe it either. Out walked Priam—unarmed, unarmored, unescorted.

HOMER

What was Hoplite's reaction?

MUSE

Agamemnon was going ballistic over the net and screamed for someone—anyone—to take Priam out. But nobody moved. Everyone just watched as Priam walked right up to Achilles and stood there. At first, I thought he would try fighting Achilles, but he didn't.

HOMER

If he didn't go out to fight, why was he there? What did he want? Did he do anything? Say anything?

MUSE

I found out later that Priam asked Achilles a question.

HOMER

Do you know what that question was?

MUSE

He said, "May I please have my son back so that my wife and I can bury our boy?"

HOMER

What was Achilles' answer?

MUSE

He was visibly moved.

HOMER

Why do you think so?

MUSE

He'd been around long enough and fought in enough battles to know that a fallen comrade couldn't always be recovered, and he'd attended too many memorial services where nothing remained of a loved one but an empty uniform in a coffin and a picture on an easel.

HOMER

Are you saying that his reaction was purely sentimental?

MUSE

Kind of. Achilles knew the importance of closure for the families of those fallen warriors. To have that one last chance to see them, to say goodbye, and to say how much they loved them. Doing so is the only way to properly mourn a death.

HOMER

Go on.

MUSE

Even though he didn't lose a son, Achilles lost his best friend in this conflict. However, Hoplite was able to recover his body, and Achilles and Myrmidon said their goodbyes and mourned. On this point, two warriors, Achilles and Priam, found common ground.

HOMER

And what was that?

MUSE

A father mourning a son. A friend mourning a friend. Two warriors respecting that the fight was done and that they needed to grieve.

HOMER

What happened next?

MUSE

In a surprisingly touching moment—so out of place with what was going on around us—Achilles and Priam embraced, showing each other love and respect from one warrior to another.

HOMER

Then what happened?

MUSE

They both knelt and placed their hands on Hector. They appeared to be praying. Those two men showed Hector the love and respect for a man who gave the last true and full measure of himself. After their prayer, Achilles picked Hector up off the ground in a fireman's carry and walked toward the Trojan safe house with Priam.

HOMER

Really?

MUSE

Yeah. We couldn't believe it either, but Priam stopped him and motioned for Achilles to give Hector to him.

HOMER

What did Achilles do?

MUSE

He carefully transferred Hector's body from his shoulders to Priam's, and the two of them walked toward the safe house. Once they were close to the entryway, Priam stopped Achilles and said something like, "I've got him from here. Thank you."

HOMER

Then what happened?

MUSE

From my drone feeds, I saw Priam carry Hector inside, and I could see Achilles standing there in the open and watching Priam disappear inside.

HOMER

That's pretty powerful stuff.

MUSE

It is. It was. And that's the end of the first event, the one no one wants to remember.

HOMER

Okay. Tell me about the second event.

MUSE

The second event happened immediately after the first event ended.

HOMER

What happened?

MUSE

Paris shot and killed Achilles.

SECTION 29

HOMER

By your own account, you said that Paris wouldn't have stood a chance against Achilles. If that's the case, then how did he manage to shoot at Achilles let alone kill him?

MUSE

Sniper shot from a concealed position. Paris was on some type of overwatch detail. He obviously saw Achilles kill his brother, and it's my theory that he planned to immediately snipe him, but then his father came out and interrupted his plan. Paris had to wait until Priam was clear before firing. Once Priam was back in the safe house, Paris executed his shot.

HOMER

Where was Achilles struck?

MUSE

Right between the eyes. He was dead before he even hit the ground.

HOMER

If the shot came from a concealed position, then how did you locate the sniper? And how did you know the sniper was Paris?

MUSE

We had sniper overwatch in place, too. We were prepared to follow a plan similar to Paris' if Hector had killed Achilles. Our overwatch was briefed to kill Hector just like I'm sure the Trojan overwatch was briefed to kill Achilles.

HOMER

Any truth to the rumor that Paris took out Achilles with an arrow?

MUSE

No. The accompanying sound was definitely from a rifle.

HOMER

Okay, so once the sniper shot came, Paris' position had been given away, and your counter-sniper fired in response, correct?

MUSE

Correct.

HOMER

How did you identify Paris as the shooter? Did you find his body?

MUSE

We found Paris' hide site and body during back-clearing operations.

HOMER

What Hoplite sniper claimed the kill?

MUSE

Philoctetes.

HOMER

The former scout sniper? Our sources indicated that he wasn't operational anymore. We thought he was only working as an instructor.

MUSE

Well, your sources are partially correct. He did sustain a pretty nasty lower-body injury during his time in service, an injury that forced him to medically retire. So, you're right in that he wasn't operational, in a sense. He pretty much only taught, but he was also brought on as a consultant anytime a contract needed scout sniper operations, or whenever there was the potential to counter an enemy sniper element.

HOMER

So, what role was he contracted to fill?

MUSE

Because of the skill and reputation of Paris and his Archers, Agamemnon brought Philoctetes on board and often placed him in an overwatch position to observe, report, advise, and assist as needed. Philoctetes wasn't out running and gunning with the other Hoplite elements. He set up a hide site providing overwatch and counter-sniper services.

HOMER

So, this whole conflict devolved into a sniper's duel?

MUSE

Paris was damn good. But Philoctetes was better, more patient. Paris probably would've survived if he had stuck to a basic sniper tenet.

HOMER

Which is?

MUSE

Shoot and move. He shot. He hit his target. But he stuck around to revel in his kill. Philoctetes could tell where the shot came from because of the dust and debris kicked up from Paris' muzzle blast. Philoctetes even caught a glint of glass that reflected off a light source. And we aren't talking about incredibly long engagement distances here. That shot by Paris was easy to spot for a master sniper like Philoctetes. The shot was even easier to return because of Paris' inattention to detail.

HOMER

So, in the span of a few moments, Hector, Achilles, and Paris all died?

MUSE

Like I said before, we didn't know that Paris had died until post-operational back clearing was underway, when his body was discovered and positively identified. But yes.

HOMER

Did Hoplite launch an immediate assault on the Trojan safehouse after the deaths of Hector, Achilles, and Paris?

MUSE

No. We could've, but there was too much confusion. Command and control were breaking down, so Agamemnon wisely ordered a tactical withdrawal.

HOMER

Agamemnon? I'm surprised. I figured he would've wanted to attack right away and not give Trojan time to regroup.

MUSE

At this point, he knew that victory was at hand. Trojan was contained. They were trapped. They weren't going anywhere. The Sons melted away, knowing that the fight was over. The Sons also knew that if they wanted to continue operating, they needed to abandon Trojan to their fate. Agamemnon knew what Priam knew.

MUSE
Which was?

MUSE

Hector was dead. Priam likely knew that Paris was dead too and that Trojan was decimated. Priam would never recover from this conflict, personally or financially. Trojan was ruined. Only one thing of value remained.

HOMER

Let me guess. Helen Argos?

MUSE

Correct. I've said this throughout our debrief because it's true: Agamemnon is many things, but stupid isn't one of them. He paid a heavy price to be where he was at this stage of the operation, and whether out of wariness or respect for an old comrade-in-arms, he wanted to give Priam one last chance to walk away alive.

HOMER

That seems very out of character for Agamemnon.

MUSE

It was. But that wasn't the only reason why Agamemnon didn't attack right away. He was taking this opportunity to once again rest, rearm, and refit his forces while simultaneously planning a surrender option for Priam. And if Priam refused to surrender, then Agamemnon had the final assault option ready to go.

HOMER

Do you know, or did you know, Priam's position on the matter?

MUSE

I have my theories, along with what we've pieced together from postoperative SSE.

HOMER

SSE?

MUSE

Sensitive site exploitation.

HOMER

Thank you. Please continue.

MUSE

Before I get into Priam's position, I think it's important to mention that Hoplite received a re-tasking order from Zeus regarding Operation Trojan War.

HOMER

What was the nature of the re-tasking?

MUSE

Once we had Priam contained, Agamemnon contacted Zeus and briefed him on the current situation. He told Zeus that Hector and Achilles had died and that the sniper who assassinated Achilles had been neutralized. Remember, at the time, we didn't know yet that the sniper was Paris.

HOMER

Okay.

MUSE

Agamemnon also requested permission to negotiate a surrender of both Helen and what remained of Trojan.

HOMER

Did Zeus agree with this proposed course of action?

MUSE

No. Zeus immediately re-tasked Agamemnon by ordering him to eliminate Helen and every single remaining member of Trojan. It didn't matter if the only ones left were trigger pullers or support staff. Zeus was clear: everyone dies.

HOMER

And Agamemnon accepted this re-tasking?

MUSE

He did; but Agamemnon being Agamemnon, he told Zeus that a re-tasking would require additional financial compensation.

HOMER

Did Zeus agree?

MUSE

Yes. I don't know the particulars of the deal, but Zeus agreed to pay extra for Hoplite's additional work.

HOMER

I want to circle back to your theory about Priam—what he was thinking and how he responded to the situation he found himself in.

MUSE

Again, this information is pieced together from what I knew at the time, along with my working theory and what we found out from intelligence afterward as part of our SSE.

HOMER

Understood. Please continue.

MUSE

Priam knew he wasn't walking out of this thing alive. He also knew that no one else in Trojan was making it out alive, either. So, he gave those people in the fortified safe house with him four choices.

HOMER

And those were?

MUSE

One, they could surrender and take their chances with Hoplite. Two, they could wait to be overrun and take their chances with Hoplite. Three, they could all commit suicide and go out on their own terms—*roll to your rifle*, that type of thing.

HOMER

And the fourth option?

MUSE

They could fight. If they were going to die anyway, at least they could take as many Hoplite operators with them as possible and go out like warriors.

HOMER

What choice was made?

MUSE

Are you aware of any prisoners taken?

HOMER

No.

MUSE

Neither am I. Trojan chose to fight and chose death before dishonor. But there was one last little "fuck you" to Agamemnon from Priam.

HOMER

What was that?

MUSE

Priam wouldn't let Helen get taken by Hoplite. He had already lost everything. His sons. His company. His reputation. His legacy. But there was no way he would lose his honor by giving Agamemnon the satisfaction of complete mission success.

HOMER

Priam was going to make this a pyrrhic victory? What did he do?

MUSE

He arranged to smuggle Helen out of his fortified safe house.

HOMER

How?

MUSE

Through an underground tunnel system that we weren't aware of until post-operation activities.

HOMER

Where did Helen go, and who did she go with?

MUSE

We didn't find out the particulars until after the fact, but apparently Priam reached out to a private intelligence contractor he had worked with in the past, a contractor who owed him a favor.

HOMER

He called in a marker.

MUSE

He certainly did.

HOMER

That must have been a pretty fucking big favor to agree to smuggle Helen out with all that heat coming down.

MUSE

Blood debts will do that.

HOMER

They certainly will. Do you know the name of the contractor Priam used? And if so, what can you tell me about him?

MUSE

Her. The contractor who smuggled Helen Argos out was a woman by the name of Polyxo Rhodes.

HOMER

So, Helen got away? Damn. My agency has been trying to figure out what happened to her. We have tons of solid evidence and information about what happened to just about everyone else on both Hoplite and Trojan sides, but we have no information or leads as to her whereabouts. I can't believe she actually got away.

MUSE
She didn't.

HOMER
What? But you just said she was smuggled out.

MUSE
She was, but how much do you know about Polyxo Rhodes?

HOMER
Nothing. I'm just learning about her now.

MUSE
Her specialty is human intelligence—spotting sources, recruiting them, developing them, and working them. Moving them and hiding them. She's good at what she does. It's small-scale, but she's a professional.

HOMER
What else can you tell me about her?

MUSE
I was able to learn from her operational history that she'd done work for Trojan in the past.

HOMER
That's not unusual.

MUSE
It's not, but their relationship went even deeper.

HOMER

How deep?

MUSE

Priam saved her life on an operation that went sideways. And during the course of that rescue operation, she met a Trojan operator by the name of Lepolemus. He was one of the guys on the team that pulled her out.

HOMER

And?

MUSE

They fell in love. They got married.

HOMER

It feels like there's more to this story. What happened to him?

MUSE

He got killed during Operation Trojan War. Polyxo was in a tough spot. She hated Helen and blamed her for causing the war, and as a result, her husband's death. But she owed a life debt to Priam. She honored that debt by smuggling out the woman she hated.

HOMER

Then what?

MUSE

Once Helen was stashed in one of Polyxo's safe houses, Polyxo sent a back-channel message to Zeus and told him that she had Helen.

HOMER

What information or direction did Zeus pass back to her?

MUSE

He ordered Polyxo to kill Helen.

HOMER

Did Polyxo do it?

MUSE

She drugged Helen to make her unconscious and then hanged her to make the death look like a suicide.

HOMER

So, the motive was pure revenge? Can you expound? I need more than just revenge. Period. End of sentence. You know what I mean?

MUSE

Like I said before, Polyxo owed Priam and Trojan for saving her life on an operation gone bad, right?

HOMER

Right.

MUSE

As a result, she met her future husband. With me so far?

HOMER

I am. Go on.

MUSE

Then Paris did something stupid by double-crossing Menalaus

and bringing Helen to Priam, and by extension, to Trojan and her husband, Lepolemus.

HOMER

Continue.

MUSE

Ultimately, Polyxo blamed Paris for bringing Helen into her family's life. She also blamed Priam for not immediately turning Helen over to Zeus. Last, she blamed Helen most of all because she was the catalyst that started this whole conflict. Helen was the cause of the fighting that ultimately took her husband's life. So, Polyxo exploited an opportunity that allowed her to repay her debt to Priam while at the same time getting her hands on the person she felt was most responsible for the endless tragedies.

HOMER

And now, she had Zeus' favor by being the person who finally solved his Helen Argos problem.

MUSE

Exactly. Her plan kept her honor intact. She got her revenge, and now she had a new benefactor.

HOMER

That was going to be my next question. What did she receive from Zeus? Money? Contracts?

MUSE

Nothing.

HOMER

Nothing?

MUSE

Word around the contractor's watercooler is that she only asked for one thing—that one day, if Polyxo needed a favor, Zeus would have to say yes.

HOMER

And he agreed?

MUSE

I heard that he did.

HOMER

So, his biggest problem, Helen Argos, is taken care of, and now he has to turn his attention to his contractor problem. Trojan still needed to be dealt with. He would never allow anyone from that organization to survive and talk about what happened, correct?

MUSE

Dead men tell no tales, right?

HOMER

How did the end play out?

MUSE

It brings us back to the re-tasking of Hoplite.

HOMER

Please tell me what you know about the re-tasking.

MUSE

Once the re-tasking was accepted, Operation Trojan War officially ended, and a new operation began immediately.

HOMER

That's what I want to talk about now—that new operation, in general, and about one Trojan operator, in particular. Tell me about Operation Trojan Fall and Aeneas.

ATTACHMENT 11

BRIEFING NOTES: LAW ENFORCEMENT PRESS RELEASE

RELEVANT TEXT

FOR IMMEDIATE RELEASE

The Metropolitan Police Department has received numerous complaints of hundreds of drone sightings, along with multiple reports of heavily armed individuals wearing body armor and helmets in and around the city's industrial area.

The Metropolitan Police Department has investigated all complaints received, and we can definitively state that during our investigation, these sightings were confirmed to be part of a large-scale training exercise conducted by the federal government, along with the support and partnership of our county and state colleagues.

The Metropolitan Police Department would like to reassure the public that they are in absolutely no danger. Other sightings to date, not connected to the large-scale training exercise referenced above, can be attributed to hobbyist drones, commercial drones, and our own department drones, along with the legitimate flights of fixed and rotary-wing aircraft.

There have also been reports of celestial bodies mistakenly called in as drones.

In closing, the Metropolitan Police Department would like to reiterate that the public should not worry and that we are confident the training exercise presents no security or public safety risk.

However, out of an abundance of caution, civilians and unauthorized personnel are advised to stay out of the designated training area until the exercise is complete. Updates regarding the exercise's completion will be provided as more information becomes available.

SECTION 30

MUSE

No.

HOMER

Excuse me?

MUSE

You heard me. I said no.

HOMER

Why not?

MUSE

Correct me if I'm wrong, but I agreed to tell the truth, the whole truth, and nothing but the truth about Operation Trojan War and my involvement in that conflict, right?

HOMER

That's right.

MUSE

Have I done that?

HOMER

Yes.

MUSE

So, then I've lived up to my end of the bargain?

HOMER

You have.

MUSE

And are you going to hold up your end of the bargain?

HOMER

Of course, I am. I gave you my word.

MUSE

Okay then—we're done here. Transaction complete.

HOMER

 True, but I still need information on what happened next.

MUSE

Then find someone else and break his balls like you broke mine.

HOMER

There isn't anyone else I trust.

MUSE

What makes you think I can be trusted?

HOMER

I've been doing this job for a long time. I can tell when someone is trying to put one over on me. You never once tried to bullshit me or shine me on. You gave it to me straight. Granted, I had to redirect you a couple of times here and there, but you told me everything you knew about Operation Trojan War and even passed along your own theories. You didn't have to do that. You could've played it right down the middle. That's why I need your help.

MUSE

Why?

HOMER

Why what?

MUSE

Why are you doing this? Why are you continuing to press? You got what you wanted. Move on.

HOMER

I can't.

MUSE

Why not?

HOMER

During our debrief, I became aware of larger things at play here than what I was originally assigned to investigate. I have to follow the leads where they take me. There's no other option.

MUSE

There's always an option. Isn't that what you told me at the start of our debrief? You have a choice. Granted, that choice might not be a great one, but it's still a choice. And you haven't answered my question. Why are you continuing to pursue this case?

HOMER

I just told you. I was assigned to investigate Operation Trojan War. Additional leads have been developed. This case is still open. I have to see this through to the end.

MUSE

That's bullshit. I've been around the block a few times, too. And I've interfaced with tons of investigators, and I've read reports and transcripts from a shit ton of people who were assigned to get to the bottom of something. You could tell those guys were just going through the motions and checking the boxes. But not you. You won't let this case go. Why not?

HOMER

Because I have a duty, and the truth needs to be told.

MUSE

No matter what the cost?

HOMER

No matter the cost. All of the facts and circumstances surrounding this case—and anything peripheral to it—need to come to light.

MUSE

And you're the guy for the job?

HOMER

Who else is going to do it? You?

MUSE

Me? Hell no. I'm not the investigator here.

HOMER

Then I guess that leaves me.

MUSE

You're playing with fire.

HOMER

Duly noted.

MUSE

If you start down this road, there's no coming back. You know that, right? You've seen the lengths Zeus has taken to keep his sins hidden. And you've seen the influence that someone like Agamemnon has simply by working for Zeus. This investigation won't end well.

HOMER

You let me worry about that.

MUSE

That's easy for you to say. Do you even have the authority to pursue this matter further?

HOMER

I do.

MUSE

From whom?

HOMER

Themis.

MUSE

Really? The Lady of Justice herself? So that's how you're doing this. You're connected.

HOMER

Connected?

MUSE

Yeah. Connected. Politically juiced up. You have the backing of the highest-ranking person in the government who deals with justice. That's something we call top cover.

HOMER

Cover or no cover, it makes no difference to me. What matters is that right is right, and wrong is wrong. And innumerable wrongs were committed here. People need to be held accountable.

MUSE

The vast majority of those people are already dead. You know that, right?

HOMER

Not all of them. Some people involved in this war—and other shady operations—are still out there and need to be brought to justice. No one is above the law.

MUSE

Yeah, but what if some of those people you're gunning for are the ones who make the law?

HOMER

So what? Rules for thee, but not for me? Is that what you're suggesting? Are you okay with that level of corruption?

MUSE

No, I'm not *okay* with it. But that's how the world works. I've accepted that, and I've learned how to operate in the real world. Why haven't you?

HOMER

Because justice delayed is justice denied. No one gets a pass—no one.

MUSE

Okay.

HOMER

Okay, what?

MUSE

I'll help you.

HOMER

What? Why? What do you want in exchange?

MUSE

Two things. One is money, and we'll talk about how much later on. But the second thing is a little trickier to explain.

HOMER

What is it? What makes you want to help me now?

MUSE

I want to help you because I'm intrigued by you.

HOMER

I intrigue you? And that's the reason why you'll help?

MUSE

I've never met someone like you. As strange as it sounds, I respect you. Maybe not what you do. But I do respect your conviction. You're brave. You're noble, but not in a snotty, bitchy way.

You may even be a tad bit misguided in terms of the big picture, specifically on how the world works, but at your core, your beliefs are pure.

HOMER

Thank you. And believe it or not, I've actually come to respect you, too. Maybe I misjudged you.

MUSE

No, you haven't. I do what I do for the reasons I told you. I'm many things, but the one thing I'm not is a liar. You and I have honesty as a shared belief system. Now, our versions of honesty are different. I'm honest in that I don't lie. I'll tell you what I am going to do and why I'm doing it. Spoiler alert, it's usually for money. But you're honest in that you embody honesty as an ideal. You possess this integrity that goes way beyond not lying or cheating. That's why I'll help you on this batshit crazy war that you're so hell-bent on waging.

HOMER

Thinking back on our conversation, I know what you meant about being different sides of the same coin.

MUSE

Oh yeah?

HOMER

Yeah. You were right.

MUSE

Right about what?

HOMER

How in the end, we all get spent.

MUSE

Just remember, there's the value of something, and then there's the cost of something. If you decide to go through with this investigation, the answers will cost you everything.

END TRANSCRIPT

ATTACHMENT 12

CASE NOTES: NATIONAL PRINT MEDIA EXCERPT

RELEVANT TEXT

The political world was rocked today by the announcement that the Department of Justice would be launching a full-scale criminal investigation into allegations of criminal conspiracy, misconduct, corruption, and other unspecified criminal acts against the Commander-in-Chief and some members of his Cabinet.

Criminal proceedings against the Leader of the Free World began shortly after the release of a scathing investigative report. The lead investigator and author of the report could not be reached for comment. However, sources close to the investigator have hinted that this newly released report is possibly one of three reports graphically detailing further acts of criminal maleficence at the highest levels of government.

Attempts were made to reach the President for comment. However, according to the Press Secretary, there will be no official response or comment for the record until this matter is properly adjudicated.

Additional sources, speaking on the condition of anonymity, have speculated that this criminal investigation, and the others that are likely to follow, may be connected not only to the apparent suicide of international supermodel turned entrepreneur Helen Argos, but also to the recent, large-scale terrorism training exercise that is believed *to have resulted in the deaths of hundreds of private military, security, and intelligence contractors.*

The exact number of deaths is yet to be confirmed.

This is an ongoing story. Please stay with us as this story develops.

AUTHOR'S NOTE

I would like to thank the wonderful team at Indigo River Publishing, especially Georgette Green who took a chance on a first-time author. To Keira Lopez, who put Shelby Poulin and I together. To Shelby Poulin, whose insight and guidance helped me through the editing process. To River Chau, who welcomed me to the Indigo River Publishing family with open arms and encouragement. To Deborah Froese and Abigail Dengler, who put the finishing touches on this book. And to Emma Elzinga and her design team, who worked tirelessly behind the scenes to bring this book to life. Writing may be a solitary endeavor, but the entire editing and publishing process is most definitely a team effort. I am humbled and honored to be part of this team.

As a reimagining and retelling of Homer's *Illiad, Operation Trojan War* explores the question, *What if the events of the* Illiad *took place today?* It also asks, *Who are today's gods and heros?*

One could argue that the gods of modernity are actors, athletes, business moguls, celebrities, social media influencers, and politicians, as well as other officials in positions of power. These modern-day gods impact almost every aspect of our lives and the choices we make; much in the same way the gods of antiquity did with those who came before us.

If we've established who the gods of modernity are; then who are today's heroes? I believe it could be argued that modern society no longer has heroes because the lessons taught and learned from mythology have either been forgotten or abandoned altogether.

The mythology of the ancient world celebrated and revered the journey of the hero, who many times survived something horrific or tragic, and who vowed to overcome and persevere in order to make sure what happened to them would not happen to others. Heros of the ancient world did not wrap themselves in the cloak of victimhood. Rather, heros of old wore their pain and suffering like armor and arose victorious at the end.

This is something that appears to be missing in recent modern society. Does the hero archetype even exist anymore? If not, it should, and this is where we can still learn from the mythology of old. What type of hero do we want to be? The hero who is pure of heart? Or a tragic hero beholden to some character flaw?

Is the hero who behaves badly still a "good" person?

At one point, mythology taught people how to conduct themselves in their respective societies. Myths taught people about good and evil, right and wrong, love and hate, revenge and redemption. It is my sincere hope that by modernizing ancient mythology, these topics can once again be explored beyond the pages and panels of comic books and graphic novels to help reform the moral bedrock of society.

Old world lessons and knowledge are still applicable in our new world. Our gods may be different, and hopefully our heroes are only just hiding under the surface and not gone forever.

Writing *Operation Trojan War* was a massive undertaking. To give you something different and special, to help you to feel like you're reading something you're not supposed to read and learning things you're not supposed to know, I chose to shape this book like a classified debriefing transcript.

I hope you enjoyed reading this as much as I enjoyed writing it. Without you, this whole thing collapses in on itself. One of my favorite authors, Jack Carr, once theorized that you – the reader – are trusting the author with two things... your money and your time. I hope that both were well spent.

For my readers, consider yourselves to be "plank holders" in my modern mythology movement. Please continue with me on this journey. It's only just begun.

And last, but certainly not least, this was for the first responder community and the families of those who made the ultimate sacrifice. Never forget that their loved ones gave up all of their tomorrows for someone else's today. For my brothers and sisters who have secured and gone end of watch, rest easy, we'll take it from here.

Sincerely,

Justin I. Paquette, 2025